# FLIGHTS OF THE HERONS

## ESTHER ROYER AYERS

*To Barbara, my Royer-Royer third cousin. Finally our paths cross when we're in our seventies. How thrilled I am! How thrilled our ancestors must be!*

*Esther Royer Ayers*
*Feb. 2011*

Copyright © 2001 by Esther Royer Ayers.

Library of Congress Number: 2001116436
ISBN #:     Softcover           0-7388-6352-1

All rights reserved. No part of this book may be reproduced or transmitted in any form or by any means, electronic or mechanical, including photocopying, recording, or by any information storage and retrieval system, without permission in writing from the copyright owner.

This is a work of fiction. Names, characters, places and incidents either are the product of the author's imagination or are used fictitiously, and any resemblance to any actual persons, living or dead, events, or locales is entirely coincidental.

This book was printed in the United States of America.

Cover photo credits:
Photograph of light: © Paul E. Royer, San Francisco, California
Photograph of Herons: © Dick Barker, Port Richey, Florida

**To order additional copies of this book, contact:**
Xlibris Corporation
1-888-7-XLIBRIS
www.Xlibris.com
Orders@Xlibris.com

# CONTENTS

AUTHOR'S NOTE ............ 9

ACKNOWLEDGMENTS ............ 11

PROLOGUE ............ 13

1—A CROSSING OF PATHS ............ 15

2—LEMONADE IN THE CORNFIELD ............ 32

3—PLEIDELSHEIM ............ 50

4—CHINESE ACROBATS ............ 67

5—HANS REYHER ............ 82

6—KITTEN ............ 99

7—COMING TO AMERICA ............ 121

8—THE WEDDING ............ 139

9—THE MELTED FACE ............ 156

10—DUPED ............ 168

11—AN ACT OF KINDNESS ........................................ 173

12—THE AGREEMENT PROPOSAL ........................ 188

13—THE WILHELM FARM .......................................... 191

## DEDICATION

*This book is dedicated to Walter Elias Royer.*

## Author's Note

This book is a work of fiction; however, all genealogical references (names, dates, locations) relating to the Reyher and Wilhelm families accurately reflect known data. It should be noted that, following the practice of many new immigrants in America, Johann Gotthard Reyher "Americanized" his name—to John Royer—after his arrival in Columbiana County. His descendants have continued to use the Royer name.

Esther Royer Ayers

# Acknowledgments

Mere words could never adequately convey the heartfelt thanks I owe Frederick H. Gerlach, Ph.D., for the contribution he brought to this book. I got to know Fred, a distant cousin of mine, because of his interest in genealogy. He encouraged me to create a work of fiction that would incorporate our common genealogy. Then, empowered with excellent credentials and a first-hand knowledge of Germany (having lived there for nine years), he supplied me with the wonderful stories set in Germany and Switzerland. Throughout the writing of this book, he provided me with superb suggestions, exceptional editing help, and unsurpassed strength and support. I am profoundly indebted to him, for, without his help, this book could not have been written.

I also am indebted to Margaret Williamson Gerlach, Fred's mother (also a distant cousin). A few years ago Margaret, now deceased, manifested her love of history and family by embarking upon a genealogical quest of the Reyher family. The information she uncovered inspired Fred's stories and therefore lives in this book. Her gift and legacy will be cherished by all present and future family members.

I wish to also thank some early readers of my book and

am grateful to them for their wonderful suggestions. These readers are: Cheryl Davis, James Ayers, Jim and Doreen Ayers, Adele Goga, Carol Lange, and Marie Wareham.

Esther Royer Ayers

# Prologue

Emily Dickinson wrote:

> Hope is the thing with feathers
> That perches in the soul.

Indeed, without hope, could the human soul demand freedom and chance perilous flights to attain it?

Amateur genealogist Frank Atherton learns how the desire for freedom from oppression prompted three Reyhers to embark on perilous journeys: Hans left Switzerland for Germany in the mid-17th Century to escape the oppressive hopelessness of the post-Thirty Years' War era. His great-great-great grandson Johann emigrated to the United States to escape the political oppression of an unscrupulous German king. Now, in the modern era, Frank unexpectedly crosses the path of another oppressed Reyher, Katie, a third cousin he befriends in e-mail correspondence. The flight they come to share shows that ancestors from the distant past may be reaching out to touch future generations.

# 1

## A CROSSING OF PATHS

> There are causes—patterns in the crossing of paths—that are put together in a particular form like a snowflake, and all are different...
> — Pythagoras

On a sunny spring day in Youngstown, Ohio, a balding, paunchy Bill Krueger poked his head into the door of Frank's office. "Hi Sherri! Is Frank in yet?"

The young brunette receptionist looked up from watering the plants. Then she looked at her watch. "Not yet. I don't expect him for another half-hour. Is it urgent?"

"No, but exciting! I have something to show him. Ask him to give me a call as soon as he comes in."

Thirty minutes later Frank Atherton arrived. "Bill's looking for you," Sherri said. "He's got something exciting to show you. Said for you to call him as soon as you get in."

"H-m-m-m," said Frank, as he unlocked his desk. "I wonder what it could be?" He looked over the day's schedule. As usual, quite full. He decided it would be better to see Bill right away. He telephoned him.

Within a minute Bill arrived, enthusiastically waving a newspaper.

Frank rolled his eyes. "Just as I suspected. Something in the paper caught your interest."

Bill felt his neck hairs rise. After all, he could turn and bolt right out of the office and forget his mission. But, knowing of Frank's difficult circumstances, he ignored his irksome behavior. Instead, he asked, "Isn't your grandmother's maiden name 'Reyher'?"

Frank looked surprised. "Yes. Why do you ask? Is her name in the *New York Times?*"

No longer able to hide his irritation, Bill replied. "This is the *Morning Journal,* idiot! Columbiana's newspaper. And it's not your grandmother's name in there, but someone else's you may know. And on the front page at that!"

"*Morning Journal!* Whoa!" Frank teased his friend. "I didn't know a cosmopolitan guy like you read the regional rags."

Frank's cavalier attitude was getting under his skin. "It's **not** *my* paper," he barked. "It's Joanne's. She's from Columbiana. Went to high school there before attending Ohio State."

Frank's blue eyes misted. He said softly, "How can I forget Ohio State. That's where I met Sally."

Bill wanted to say: That's where we *all* met each other. You. Sally. Me. Joanne. Remember! But, noting the change in Frank's mood, he decided it best to simply add, "That's how it is with small-town graduates. They cling to their classmates. This 'rag'—as you so disdainfully call it—comes out every day. Believe me, we don't get dinner at our house until Joanne's digested every word in it.

"I never read it, of course, since it contains only local stuff. Happenings with friends and neighbors, school news, prep sports, that sort of thing. You have to be from the area to appreciate it.

"Anyhow, I'm immersed in an article in the *Times* on the dangers of derivatives when Joanne jumps up from her chair and shrieks: 'You'll never believe it! We have somebody famous who grew up in Columbiana!'

"'Read this!' she orders, as she thrusts the paper into my face. I thought perhaps a classmate's daughter had won a local dance contest. Something modest like that can get Joanne all excited.

"But, amazingly enough, there really *was* something interesting in the article—more, in fact, than Joanne had imagined. It was about a former local girl who had won a prestigious literary award. The girl's name was Katie Reyher Krauss!

"Reyher, Frank, Reyher! As soon as I saw that name, I recognized it as one you had put into your genealogy program—*repeatedly*, while you were in your learning mode. That's why the name stuck. Anyhow, since it's an unusual one, I thought this gal might be a relative of yours. Here! See for yourself."

His curiosity aroused by now, Frank took the paper and began to read: "Former Columbiana Girl Wins Prestigious Award." The article indicated that Katie Reyher Krauss, formerly of Columbiana, had won the William Faulkner Creative Writing Award for her short story entitled "Butterflies at Christmas."

According to the article, the winning story poignantly captured the feelings of an older woman who would be spending her first Christmas alone. She feared loneliness and tears. One day while shopping she saw a Painted Lady butterfly kit and bought it. She decided to time the propagation process so the butterflies would emerge from their chrysalises on Christmas day. Watching and caring for her butterflies kept her so busy, that, to her amazement, Christmas passed and she had not once felt lonely. She then realized her fear was not of being alone—but no longer being needed.

The citation noted Ms. Krauss now resided in Cabot,

Arkansas, with her husband Kenneth and college-age daughter, Kristine.

Frank rubbed his chin. His eyes lingered on the short blurb as he wondered what in the story had touched him so deeply. Of course, the loneliness!

He brushed a lock of dark hair from his face. Oh, the loneliness.

The story caused a fluttering within his chest, as if his heart had netted a butterfly. Adrenaline raced throughout his body, awakening long dormant schoolboy feelings. What insight and sensitivity Katie must possess to have captured loneliness in such a simple story! Frank flushed, as it flashed him back to his first encounter with Sally.

Suddenly, remembering that Bill was watching him, Frank cleared his throat and, still staring at the article, managed to mutter, "I'm sure she must be related to me somehow. As far as I know, all the Reyhers from Columbiana descend from my great-great-grandfather, Johann Gotthard Reyher."

"Thanks, Bill," he added, this time more brightly. "Thanks to both you and Joanne for finding this. Can I keep it? I'll look this woman's name up in my genealogy data tonight."

"Sure, keep it. And good luck! Boy, am I glad you got into that genealogy stuff! I was beginning to wonder about you. Wonder? Hell, no. I was worried *sick* about you, wallowing at home in your solitude since Sally's death. You'll never get over it unless you get out of your four walls. Go dancing. Go to singles clubs. Get yourself laid! Whatever you do, get off your butt and play ball!"

Bill then glanced at his wrist. "It's later than I thought. Time to start my day. See you at lunch."

Frank closed his eyes and rubbed his forehead. The mere mention of Sally's name by someone else flooded his body with emotion. Would this oppressive syndrome ever end? After all, it had been sixteen months and four days since her awful crash.

He could still hear the caller say, "She hit a tree and smashed up the car. She's been taken to St. Elizabeth's emergency room. Go quickly!"

He rushed to her side, unprepared for what he saw. She, lying on a gurney, her once beautiful face now bloodied, swollen, cuts everywhere, an ear torn off, teeth missing. Doctors labored over her, performed CPR, looked at him, then shook their heads.

Overwhelmed with nausea, he left the room, unable to say good-bye to his best friend. He felt miserably guilty about it now. But to have seen her transformed from a stunning beauty into a heaped pile of bloodied flesh and bones was more than he could endure. He should have been able to handle it. Instead, he had run out of the room, leaving her, in parts, behind to die.

He recalled books he had read on death. Was it true, he wondered, that the spirit hovered above the corpse right after death? What if Sally had been there *in spirit?* Hovering. Watching him. Waiting to be touched. Caressed. Kissed. Longing to hear the words "I love you" one last time. Instead, she had seen him bolt from the room. Now there was no way he could undo the damage.

The ensuing days were the darkest of his life. There was a funeral. Had he planned it? He could recall only that his children were there. And his grandchildren, her family, his family, friends, neighbors, colleagues, acquaintances. Hugs, kisses, crying, words of sympathy. Had it all happened to someone else? He sometimes thought so. He stood beside his body as a numb bystander in his desire to remain strong for his family.

As they lowered her into the grave, he comforted his children. And wiped the tears from his grandchildren's eyes and held them close. Then they returned to their homes, and for the first time, he was alone. The strong "numb bystander" disappeared as he again entered his world of consciousness.

Having reflected back to those days of numbness, Frank gradually grasped intuitively what he had once learned in a psychology class: his mind had shut down to protect his body from a pain it could not handle. "But what about now?" he asked his brain reproachfully. Couldn't it see that his pain was *still* unbearable? Why should it *ever* have reopened to the pain lurking there? Foolish, foolish brain.

For him day and night had become indistinguishable, as if he were in a perpetual solar eclipse. He remembered reading about the ancient Egyptians and their belief that, when the sun set for the night, it boarded a boat and sailed through an underground waterway. They called it their "underground Nile." The boat picked up the sun in the west, then dropped it off in the east the next morning. Frank was certain the boat had gotten stuck somewhere in that underground Nile.

His family, friends and colleagues saw the darkness in him. They fixed him up with dates. "You need to get out," they said. "Get other people in your mind."

He followed their suggestions, and dutifully took women to dinners, to shows, to night clubs. While dancing, he hoped desperately to feel the "full throb" he had experienced with Sally—a throb that enveloped his entire body, starting with no more than a loving glance and ending passionately under the sheets. It never happened.

The women suffocated him with shallow conversation. He watched his dates flip their hair, blot their lips, and adjust their legs provocatively. They crowed about their latest adventures: a trip to Paris, two weeks in Cairo. Yet when he asked them about the Eiffel Tower or the Egyptian Museum, the blank look on their faces betrayed them. All they had really done on their trips was shop.

When he took them home, they paused conventionally

at the door, then said, "Oh, please, come in." He and his date had a drink, and went to bed.

But the pillow talk—the whole experience in fact—was stultifying. His soul starved for synergy. He longed for someone who could fill the void in his life, the void that Sally had left. Someone who was *really* interested in him, who shared his values. But he found no one.

He decided it would be better to remain single and celibate for the rest of his life than settle for anything less than he had with Sally. A body and soul relationship. Where cells intermeshed in climax. He savored that in Sally. He required that in a relationship.

He regretted he had never pursued typical male activities, like playing golf, or hunting and fishing. He had been too wrapped up in his studies and then in his work. After marrying and starting a family, he spent all his scarce free time with Sally and the children, attending ball games, school functions, operas, ballets, art auctions. Now, at fifty-six, he considered himself too old to learn "guy games." Maybe golf one day, he thought. When he retired.

It was nearly 7 p.m. when Frank finished for the day. He drove his late-model green Saab down street after street of large colonials and finally into his driveway.

He should sell "their" house, but couldn't bring himself to do it. Instead, he rationalized constantly. In what other house would he know where everything was? His martini glass. His coffee cup. His robe. It gave him comfort to know he could find anything he wanted, even in the dark.

At times, in a fit of self-awareness, he recalled the real reason for staying put. He was afraid to get rid of anything that reminded him of Sally. Afraid that, without the sensory stimuli the house provided, he would lose his wonderful memories.

Frank entered the house, then disabled the alarm system. He performed his decompression ritual—shedding his coat and tie, checking the mail and answering machine, washing his hands—and realized that he should eat something. He looked into the refrigerator and found a pizza left over from the night before. He could have popped it into the microwave, but it didn't interest him. He wasn't hungry anyway. He'd eat later—*if* he remembered.

How much had he lost in the past year and half? Twenty pounds at least. All that extra baggage he had once carried. *Comfort fat*—his term for what others called "love handles." Fat associated with being comfortable with one's life. At that time, he rationalized that being perfectly happy and content was healthier than exercise.

After Sally's death, he exercised a bit. He managed a four-mile jog twice a week. But it was a chore, nothing he enjoyed. Although he now had the time, he lacked motivation.

Tonight there was an entirely different reason for his lack of appetite. His mind focused on Katie Reyher Krauss. Was she in his family tree? He thought so, but had to see for sure.

"Thank you, Bill," he said out loud, startling the inattentive room as he booted up his computer. Bill Krueger had been responsible for his interest in genealogy. It had all started about six months ago.

***

"What are you doing?" Bill asked on the phone.

"Nothing," Frank told him.

That did it. A half hour later Bill knocked on Frank's door. "We're going shopping," he announced.

At the store, Bill wasted no time. "Get this one!" he ordered his friend emphatically, and, before Frank could inspect what he had paid for, they were on their way home, into the house and into the den, where Bill turned on the computer. Again Frank could not keep up—this time with what was happening on his monitor. Within less than a minute, Bill had installed "Family Tree Maker."

"What's this?" asked Frank.

"A genealogy program, Frank. I've had it with your sitting around at home doing nothing, so I decided to do something about it. You're an intellectual type who studied in Europe and all of that. So I figured maybe you'd like to try genealogy. Even I've gotten into it a bit.

"Now, let's let your family tree grow. Watch how I do this! Start with your name, Sally's name, then your son Mathew and his wife Connie, their two boys—I forget their names.

"Now your daughter Melissa, husband Mike, and they have a daughter and son, right? What are their names?"

Frank told him.

"Okay, now you do it!" Bill said, motioning Frank to take his place in front of the monitor. "You can hunt and peck with the best of us. Enter your grandparents' names, paternal over here, maternal over in that branch."

Frank typed in their names, hesitated, then turned to Bill. "Would you believe it? I've forgotten my grandmother's maiden name. I'll have to call my mother. I know I've heard it, but it escapes me at the moment."

Frank picked up the phone and hit the autodial button, then one. He loved these gadgets and marveled over the developments in the telephone in his own lifetime.

"Hi Mom," he said. "Bill shanghaied me into a quick shopping trip tonight, and we bought this genealogy program. Now he's helping me to get started. I've put in a bunch of names but can't seem to remember Grandma's maiden name."

"You're getting into genealogy, Frank? That's wonderful!" Frank beamed as the little boy in him took pleasure in her praise.

His mother continued, "Her maiden name was Reyher.

She once told me it means 'heron' in German. Her grandfather, Johann Gotthard Reyher, came to America from Germany."

"Reyher. That's right. Sure. I remember. It slipped my mind for a moment."

"Oh, and one thing, Frank. When your grandmother passed away, she left a large envelope. Since I'm an only child, naturally everything came to me. It's marked 'genealogy stuff.' It has a lot of names and other information. If you're getting into genealogy, it's yours."

"Great, Mom. I'll pick it up tomorrow after work."

"Stay for dinner, won't you? We'll be great company for each other. I'm tired of going out with my lady friends. All of us are widows. I need a change of conversation."

"I'd love to, Mom. See you around six then."

"It's 'Reyher,'" Frank told Bill after hanging up. "I should have remembered it."

"That's an odd name. What kind of a name is that?"

"It's German for 'heron.' Spelled R-e-y-h-e-r," said Frank as he entered the name in its proper place. "Mom says she has all sorts of genealogy information. I'm going to pick it up tomorrow evening."

"Great! So maybe next time when I call, you won't tell me you're doing nothing."

"For the next few days, that's a fair assumption," Frank chuckled. "Thanks for your help."

"No problem. It's getting late, and I promised Joanne I'd not be gone long, so I'll see you tomorrow, Frank. Have fun!"

The next evening Frank reveled in roast pork with all the fixings—mashed potatoes, gravy, sweet corn, green peas, and roasted apples. What a feast! As he wiped his mouth with his napkin, his eyes twinkled merrily in the knowledge that his mother was attempting, in one meal, to provide him with all the vitamins and minerals his body needed for the next month. A mother still nurturing her child.

After dinner, they sipped sherry and talked about his work

and her many current activities. As he got up to leave for home, his mother tucked the envelope from Grandma Reyher under his arm.

Later Frank opened the envelope. The contents captivated him: records kept meticulously for years, decades. They began with the name of Johann Gotthard Reyher, who was born somewhere in Germany in 1798 and then emigrated to America, arriving at the port of Philadelphia in 1819. The young man eventually settled in the Columbiana area of eastern Ohio, worked for a farmer, and ultimately married the farmer's daughter, a "Katharina Wilhelm." A few years later, Johann bought the farm from his father-in-law. It was located in Beaver Township, just outside the Columbiana town limits, and faced Old Salem Road, also known as Route 14.

The records listed all of Johann and Katharina's children, *their* spouses and *their* children. Generation after generation. All carefully hand-written by Grandma, who probably was working from documents she had seen or from stories she had been told. He could imagine her sitting beside the fireplace, laboriously, but lovingly, adding the names of the newborn children, perhaps his first, second, even third cousins. Frank saw his name, Sally's, their children's and grandchildren's names, his sister Susan's whole family. Dates and places of birth. For the deceased, dates of death and often even burial locations too. There were amazingly few gaps. All done for him! Ready for computerization. For inputting into his genealogy program.

Frank wondered where exactly in Germany Johann Gotthard had come from and what circumstances had prompted him to leave for the New World.

"Maybe I could look into that," Frank said out loud, startling the room again. After all, he had taken several years of German and at one time thought about making a career of it. Maybe his mother would help with the research. He'd call her in the morning.

Better yet, why not visit Germany? Everyone was urging him to take a vacation, and he needed one. And maybe Mom would like to go along! Together they would search for answers to open questions. An ancestral adventure! Retracing the steps of young Johann. What a tonic for the dull johnnie that Frank had become!

When Frank broached the subject with his mother the next day, she instantly bought into it. By that evening they had visited a travel agency and arranged for a trip in the middle of May.

In the ensuing weeks and months, genealogy consumed Frank. Even his elderly mother got caught up in the fervor. After entering all the data from Grandma's records, he joined his mother in an aggressive search for new information wherever they could find it. They visited libraries, historical societies, and Mormon genealogy research centers. They "internetted" *ad nauseum*, and Frank read extensively about relevant areas of European history.

Although his command of the German language was still excellent years after the college courses in the subject, he decided to refresh his skills at the local university. "I want to get as much as possible out of this trip," he confided to his mother. "Who knows? Maybe I'll write a book on this someday. It certainly is fascinating material."

\*\*\*

As Frank prepared to look up Katie's name in the genealogy files, he ruminated over the coincidence of the award announcement and his trip to Germany scheduled in only two weeks. Had fate caused his path to cross Katie's in such a unique way at this time? Frank didn't believe in predestination. But sometimes he had to wonder. Could an event this singular have resulted from sheer chance?

He put these thoughts aside for now as he concentrated

on the task at hand: seeing whether Katie was related to him. He booted up his Gateway computer and clicked onto the Family Tree Maker icon. Everything moved at a speed that once would have amazed him, but now left him impatient. His two-year-old computer had fallen far behind in the race. For some reason, he recalled his mother's tale about "Uncle Joe" who had loudly proclaimed fifteen miles per hour as the fastest any car should be allowed to go. With his computer, he was in danger of becoming an Uncle Joe.

Into the program at last, he perused the lengthy list of Reyhers. Search. Search. Finally, he found a "Katharina Reyher." He clicked on that name and then onto another icon to look at her pedigree.

Eureka! There she was, a great-great-granddaughter of Johann Gotthard Reyher!

Now what would that make their relationship? Click. Click.

Of course, third cousins! Frank jumped up from his chair. Katie and he shared Johann Gotthard and Katharina Wilhelm as great-great-grandparents! More than he could have hoped for! From deep within, he felt a pleasant twinge as the dark clouds parted and a resplendent rainbow shot an arrow tipped with sunshine into his heart.

He sat at his computer again and caught his breath. He looked at the name on his screen and contemplated about whether Katie knew any of the fascinating information he had uncovered so far on Johann. All of a sudden the events of his momentous day effervesced within him, like freshly poured champagne. Words opened his mouth and effused from his lips. "Wait 'til Mom hears this!"

Frank immediately telephoned his mother with the news of how Bill had burst into his office that morning with a Columbiana newspaper article about a literary award to a girl named Katie Reyher and how she had wonderfully written about an older woman and Christmas and butterflies and everything. "And guess what, Mom! I checked my data, and Katie's there. We're related! We're third cousins!"

"Do you still have her name on your screen?" his mother asked.

"Yes, why?"

"Count how many children were in the family, Frank."

"Twelve. I count twelve."

"That's what I was afraid of. Before you get too carried away, you should know that family was from the Old Order Mennonite religion. The Reyhers generally are Lutheran, or don't practice any religion. However, this one Reyher boy fell in love with an Old Order Mennonite girl and married her. Your grandmother told me about them. She had seen their births listed in the newspaper. Otherwise, we wouldn't have known. People in that religion tend to keep to themselves.

"This Reyher fellow died thirty or so years ago, which your grandmother noted. Anyway, a few years after his death, we saw an ad in the paper where the family was selling the farm, the equipment, everything. Later, someone told us they moved out of the state.

"Frank, Old Order Mennonites don't go any further in school than the eighth grade. How could someone from that background win a prestigious writer's award? I don't see how the Katie you're talking about could have come from this family."

Only then did it dawn on Frank: He had simply *assumed* the "Katharina" in his computer to be the "Katie" in the *Morning Journal* article. He whispered a curse, taking care, as usual, that his mother didn't hear him.

But his logic took only a brief time-out.

"Mother, how many Katie Reyhers from Columbiana could there be? And don't you see, she must have been named after Katharina Wilhelm, Johann's wife. I'm sure 'Katie' is a nickname for Katharina. I don't know how she got from Old Order Mennonite to being a writer, but it *has* to be the same girl.

"Besides, according to our records Katharina would be forty-five, and this Katie, the writer, would be about that age since the paper said she has a daughter attending college. She lives in Cabot, Arkansas. I have already looked it up on the map. It's a small town a little northeast of Little Rock. I'll find her address using my Internet reference service. Then I'm going to write her."

"Well, good luck, Frank." His mother obviously remained skeptical, but refrained from saying anything more that might undermine the infectious enthusiasm she loved in her son, but had not witnessed for a long time.

They said good-bye and Frank hung up. He assumed, correctly, that there probably were not a lot of Krausses living in Cabot. In fact, his Internet "white pages" yielded only one: a Kenneth Krauss, the same name attributed by the newspaper story to Katie's husband. No doubt about it, Frank concluded. He had located the writer Katie Krauss. Now to find out whether she was the Katharina in his genealogy data! He had to write her.

Frank clicked on his word-processing program. He agonized over how best to approach Katie. Should he address her as "Mrs. or Ms. Krauss?" But assuming, as he did, that she *was* his cousin, wouldn't that be excessively formal? Why not go with "Katie?" After all, this was America, where practically everyone was on a first-name basis. And calling her Katie would enable him to tell her how much he liked the name.

And how should he *end* the letter? He remembered once being told that "Sincerely" was less formal than "Sincerely yours." Maybe he should go with "Your cousin." No, that was too presumptuous. What if, contrary to his expectations, they weren't related? It would be better to stick with something innocuous.

Finally, after an unusually long labor, his letter to Katie was born.

> Dear Katie,
>
> First of all, let me congratulate you on winning the William Faulkner Creative Writing Award. Columbiana's newspaper, the "Morning Journal," summarized your story and I am touched by your insight into the life of another person. But I must be honest and tell you that your name is what really caught my attention.
>
> My maternal grandmother's maiden name was Reyher, and I have recently been working on the genealogy of the Reyher family. Naturally, when I saw your name, my interest was aroused. In my data, which I now have on computer, I found a Katharina Reyher who is from a family of twelve.
>
> My mother remembered a family of Reyhers belonging to the Old Order Mennonite religion who moved away from the Columbiana area thirty or so years ago. The newspaper article indicated you had lived in Columbiana at one time, and that you have a daughter in college. Putting available information together, I convinced myself that you are the Katharina "Katie" Reyher I've been looking for. If so, you are my third cousin!
>
> This Katharina (you) and I share a fantastic story. Our gutsy great-great-grandfather, Johann Gotthard Reyher, in 1819 slipped out of Germany without the legally required government authorization. He wanted to avoid being drafted and "exported" as a mercenary, a common practice of kings in those days to expand the revenues of their realms. When Johann safely reached Amsterdam, he made a deal with the captain of a ship destined for Philadelphia. In return for his ocean passage he indentured himself for several years in America.
>
> A lot of the early information—the names, dates of

birth, etc.—*came from my maternal grandmother. But for additional details and background, my mother and I have been doing research like crazy over the past few months. There is still lots more to learn: where exactly in Germany Johann came from, for example. So, to find out about this and anything else available about our ancestry, my mother and I are planning to visit Germany in a couple of weeks.*

*It had been my intent to gather all this information and someday write a book about it. However, when I realized that you and I have a common ancestry, at least I assume we do, I thought how much better it would be to collaborate on a book with an already-established writer—you!*

*I hope you will not think I am too forward in approaching you this way, but I also hope you will be interested. If you are, I am sure we can easily work out a satisfactory arrangement. I can hardly wait to hear from you!*

*In closing, I want to tell you how much I like your name.*
Sincerely,
*Frank Atherton*
*P.S.—Incidentally, are you aware that Reyher means "heron" in German?*

Frank printed the letter on his best available paper stock, signed it, and on his way to work the next morning made a detour to post it in the early pick-up box.

# 2

## LEMONADE IN THE CORNFIELD

Katie limped to the mailbox. The typical contents—bills, advertisements, her *Psychology Today*, and several mail-order catalogs—concealed a letter that would transform her day.

As she kept a watchful eye on the chicken pot, she sorted the mail on the kitchen table. "For me, for Ken, for the 'circular file.'"

Then, she noticed something odd. What was this? A letter addressed to her from a Frank Atherton? She didn't know anyone by that name. And from Youngstown? Who could that be?

She assumed the letter had something to do with her award, for she was aware an announcement and summary of the short story had recently appeared in the Columbiana paper. Her local paper, the *Cabot Star Herald*, had published the entire story.

Although she had received many congratulatory letters and phone calls from the Cabot and Columbiana areas, to have one come from Youngstown, and from someone she didn't know, puzzled her.

She stirred the chicken pot, then sat at the table and opened the envelope. "Dear Katie," she read.

The further she got, the more she felt inexplicably strengthened by the letter. By the time she read, "Sincerely, Frank Atherton," an apple pie warmth enveloped her body.

She reread the statement where he said he liked her name. *He likes my name.* The unknown man from Youngstown had written so few words, yet words that spoke volumes. If he only knew how important it was for her to read them!

And yet, there was something else she detected in his letter. A tenderness came through, like soft sashes of silk tossed her way. So unlike the rough ropes of hemp that now bound her.

Oblivious to the boiling pot, she nestled his letter against her chest. Memories from the corners of her brain crept into her conscious mind, memories of a softer, gentler time. She was swept away to an August day, a busy farming day—but for the briefest time—as the sound of a car pulling into the driveway abruptly jolted her back into the present.

The garage door opened. "Uh-oh! Kenneth? Already?"

Hurry! Hurry! Hide the letter! But where? *Where?*

There, in the cupboard! Under the plates! The two bottom ones! She took a deep breath, as she contemplated her close call.

"Hi Kitten," said Ken, as he entered the kitchen and planted a big kiss on her lips. "Did you have a good day? I smell chicken and dumplings. My favorite. You sure know how to make me happy. How long before dinner?"

"It's almost ready. A half-hour at the most."

"Then I have time for a quick martini, maybe two. I've had a great day. Finally got that yogurt account. Oh, by the way, I thought you said you didn't have to go anywhere today. I see your car's been moved."

"That's what I thought when you left this morning, but then I realized I was out of celery. Chicken stock is so bland without it. I went to Templeton's. Nowhere else."

"Oh, okay, fine, no problem, just wondering. Half-hour. It sure smells good."

"Congratulations on the yogurt account," Katie said. "I know how long you've worked to get it. I'm very happy for you."

"Thanks!" said Ken. "I'll just get out of this monkey suit, then fix us a drink. You'll join me, won't you? It's a celebration, after all."

As Ken left the kitchen, Katie fumed. A celebration indeed! For *his* achievement. What about a celebration for *her* award? This guy Frank in Youngstown had congratulated her and so had plenty of others. Kristine had called from Ouachita Baptist. What a kind-hearted, considerate daughter she had! Too bad she had decided to take summer courses; otherwise, she'd still be at home.

Everybody had congratulated her. Except her own husband. He hadn't even read the story!

Tears fell down her cheeks. It was always the same. He allowed her to write because it kept her occupied—out of his hair so to speak—so that he could do "big things." Important work. Like getting the yogurt account. She had to face the truth. Her writing simply wasn't important to him.

How about *her*, she wondered. Was *she* important to Ken?

Oh, sure he *needed* her. He needed a servant to clean his house and cook his meals. He needed a mistress for sexual duties. He needed someone to escort for required social engagements. But when it came to her writing—the very essence of her being—she had to admit that Ken never saw beyond his skin walls.

She heard Ken fixing the drinks and quickly dried her eyes. She joined him in the great room. They clicked glasses. To switch her mind into a different mode, she again congratulated Ken on the new contract.

From their seats at the bar, they watched the late afternoon golfers tee off. Distant laughter reverberated in the cool air. The foursome soon finished their long wood shots, then started off in their motor carts to search for poorly positioned balls. Before the search, invariably one or two looked over at the Krausses' house. Although they were too far away to be clearly visible, Katie was sure she could read their lips: "That house is gorgeous! Wow! Wish we had the bucks to live there!"

The majestic house, with white clapboard siding and green trim, faced Mt. Carmel Road. An outside porch gloatingly ran around the front and two sides of the house. The back was practically all glass and afforded stunning views of the Rolling Hills Golf Course.

It might seem quite reckless and dangerous to put so much glass in a house that abutted a golf course. In fact, the placement of their house was such that golf balls were always driven in a direction opposite from their glass windows.

After watching the golfers, Katie felt guilty about her thoughts in the kitchen. Hadn't Ken provided well for her? When she needed money, all she had to do was ask. He usually gave her whatever she wanted. For her house, her wardrobe, her personal needs.

Indeed, anyone focused on wood and steel instead of flesh and bones would have envied Katie's station.

After dinner Katie cleaned up the kitchen while Ken played "battles of the world." *Bang, bang, zing, zing,* the noises leaped from the computer and searched out her ears. A shiver ran up and down her spine as the sounds exacted a space in her brain.

As she wiped the last dish, Ken came into the kitchen and asked, "What would you like to watch on television tonight?"

It was rerun season and they had watched all of the permissible shows during the regular season. Katie thought she might enjoy "Murphy Brown," but she knew that merely to suggest watching it was to invite criticisms and rants. It was easier to just go along. "Whatever you want," she said.

They watched a few of his shows and the late news, then

went to bed. Katie wasn't sleepy, however. Her mind was on the letter. She waited until Ken's breaths were even, his body still, then slipped out of bed and returned to the kitchen.

She carefully retrieved Frank's letter from its hiding place, sat at the table, and reread it. It pleased Katie that Frank was taking his mother to Germany. He must cherish her.

Just as she cherished her mother. And had cherished her father.

Thoughts came quickly and returned her to a hot, dry day in mid-August, when she was eight.

\*\*\*

Farm aromas from horses and threshing machines filled the air. Dry straw and stray wheat grains enjoyed a brief swirl before falling to the ground. Katie looked out of the window while drying the dishes. She could hardly see the men or their machines at work in the fields, so thick was the dust they stirred up.

She dried her last dish, then remembered her mother was making her a new school dress. That always made her happy, for most of her dresses were legacies of five older sisters. Joy turned feet to feathers as she flew into the dining room where Mama was busy at her sewing machine.

The machine whirred as Mama pressed lightly on the pedal. Then she looked up at Katie and laughed, for the pedal, along with the portable accessory motor, were new toys for her. The two units had magically converted her clang-clang, muscle-consuming Singer into an easily-operated humming machine.

Katie marveled at how quickly she pulled and seamed section after section of garment. In and out, in and out went the threaded needle as the pressure foot and feed plate joined in marriage. It was nothing for a finished garment to be born in a single afternoon under Mama's skillful guidance.

"Do you know where Rebecca is, Mama? She said she wanted to play house with me this afternoon."

"I sent her to the chicken house to water the new peeps, since your older sisters had to cook dinner for the threshers. But don't run off just yet. I have this dress just about ready to hem. A few more stitches on the waist and you can try it on."

The gingham dress material had tiny red and green checks that blended into a rather sickly brown when viewed from a distance. Drab colors like the others Katie wore. But the young girl, unaware of the effect of distance, saw only the reds and greens. The colors pleased her.

Mama held up the dress. "There, Katharina. How do you like it?"

The collarless dress had a snap at the neckline, several more snaps down the front to the waist, long sleeves, a long gathered skirt, no lace, no rickrack. Just like all her others. Katie frowned, for she was now old enough to be aware of the pretty clothing worn by her classmates.

Suddenly she had an idea. "Wouldn't this dress be pretty with some nice red and green buttons down the front?"

Mama looked at the dress, then at her. "Katharina, you have to realize that we're just a bunch of plain chickens."

No sooner had the words left her mouth when she realized how funny they sounded. Her entire body shook with laughter. When she finally gained her composure, she said, "My, that's funny! To think of us as a bunch of plain chickens. Whatever put that thought into my head?"

The image of a chicken wearing a black bonnet and black stockings made Katie laugh as well. What a funny scene that would be!

Then a vision of roosters entered her mind, and she remembered *they* didn't have to wear such dull colors. "What about plain roosters, Mama? Papa and the boys get to wear store-bought overalls, sometimes even store-bought shirts. I never get anything store-bought."

"Katharina, there's one thing you'll have to learn as you grow up. In our religion men are the head of the church and the house. It says so in our church rules. When you get married someday, you'll have to obey your husband. Whatever he says goes."

Katie rolled up her nose at that thought.

"Because men are the head, be careful who you marry. Your father is gentle and kind. Not all 'roosters' are. Remember that when you get married."

"I won't get married then," said a determined Katie. "I don't want anybody bossing me around."

"You have to get married, Katharina. You have to get married to have a baby. Roosters are the ones that give you a baby. I see you playing with your dolls. You'll be a good mother. You'll want to get married someday."

"But how, Mama? How do roosters give me a baby?"

"Oh, Katharina," Mama laughed, "you ask way too many questions for a girl of your age. I'll just tell you for now that they have a secret thing, and they use that to give you a baby."

"Is it on the tail, Mama?"

"Whatever makes you ask that?"

"Because, whenever you cut off a chicken's head, you leave the tail. But when you cut off a rooster's head, you cut off the head **and** the tail. Why do you do that?"

"Because a rooster's tail makes the soup spoil. That's why I cut it off. That's enough questions for now. Let me finish pinning the hem. Then I want you to take your father some cool lemonade before you chase down your sister."

"Where is Papa anyway? I thought he was resting in bed."

"He should be resting. The heat of the afternoon sun. It's not good for him with his white blood and all. His doctor told him that just because he feels better, it doesn't mean he's well. His disease is still in him. It will come back.

"But he refuses to take it easy. Puts on his straw hat and goes out to the garden. Pulls weeds one day, hoes the next. Today he's hoeing the sweet corn. I can't stop him."

"I'll take him some lemonade right away, Mama."

She poured cold lemonade into a galvanized gallon can, secured the lid, then tied a tin cup to the top handle.

On her way to the cornfield she passed her flowers. They made a glorious display at this time of year. She fondly remembered Mama giving her a packet of mixed flower seeds the beginning of May. "Plant the first two garden rows that face Old Salem Road," said Mama. "Plant them there so the flowers can be enjoyed by everyone who goes up and down our road. Flowers are smiles from God. They lighten the hearts of people and make this world pretty."

Vibrant pink, red, yellow, and white heads of zinnias, freesias, snapdragons and petunias nodded their thanks to Katie as she passed by. Her color-starved eyes drank in their beauty. She wondered why, if flowers were truly God's smiles, she couldn't have them on her dress. Wouldn't that lighten hearts and make people happier? Her religion had some rules that made no sense to her.

She entered the back garden and couldn't see Papa anywhere. The corn was tall, so she looked up and down each row. Finally she found him. He was lying flat on his back on the ground, his hoe beside him.

"Papa," she called, as she ran toward him. "What's wrong? Why are you on the ground?" She noticed how pale he looked.

"I'm resting, Katie," he said weakly, almost a whisper. "I got tired."

"Here, Papa. I've brought you some lemonade."

She poured some into the cup, then lifted his head just a little so that he could easily sip. After a couple of sips, she felt his head relax in her hand.

"There, doesn't that make you feel better?"

"Thanks, Katie," came his feeble reply. "It's nice."

"Oh, don't talk, Papa. You need to save your energy. Here, have some more. It'll make you stronger."

She gave him as much as he wanted. When he indicated he had enough, she gently placed his head upon the ground and said, "I'll lie in this next row, Papa. I see we have freshly tilled and raked soil today. My favorite kind. It's so warm and sweet. I feel so good whenever I lay upon freshly raked soil."

Was that a chuckle she heard arise from Papa's throat? Whatever it was, it meant approval, so she continued to talk until her voice faded and she fell asleep.

When she awoke, Papa was standing, although still pale. He supported himself with his hoe. "I think I've worked enough for today," he said.

Katie quickly got up and brushed the earth from her long blond braids. She wondered whether lying in the sun had made her freckles pop out again. She should have worn her sun bonnet, but had forgotten it in her haste to get the lemonade. She shook the remaining soil from her dress, then straightened her skirt. She was glad it was summer and she didn't have to wear shoes and those awful black stockings.

She picked up the cup and offered Papa more sips of lemonade. She noticed he straightened his shoulders a little, as if he had been strengthened by the drink.

"Katie," he said, "Let's go back to the house. But first, promise me you won't tell Mama that you found me lying in the field. She worries too much about me as it is."

"But Papa, she says the doctor said your white blood will come back. Is that true, Papa?"

"See what I told you. Your mother worries too much. The doctor told me my red blood is coming back. He told me it's much improved."

He took Katie's hand and they walked slowly, silently toward the house.

# FLIGHTS OF THE HERONS

\*\*\*

The hall clock struck one. Katie was surprised that so much time had passed while she reminisced. Frank's letter brought back such sweet memories of her childhood. She would definitely answer it.

But *how* would she respond? She noted his telephone number on the letterhead. She could call him. But then the number would appear on their monthly telephone bill. Ken would question it. She couldn't take that chance.

What if she wrote him a letter? No. Frank's response might come on a day when Ken got the mail. He would accuse her of carrying on correspondence behind his back. She couldn't chance that either.

She looked at the letterhead again. Then she noticed an e-mail address. What if she responded by e-mail? But she used Ken's program and address. She could erase her own outgoing e-mails, but Ken could retrieve and read any incoming ones. She'd have to account for such sneaky actions.

What she needed was a secret post-office box. Ken would know nothing about it, and she could clandestinely receive all of Frank's letters. But wait! People would notice all those visits she'd make to the post office checking for a letter in her box. People would talk.

Her mind darted from that idea to a conversation she recently had with Carol, her best friend. "I'm using an e-mail program called Juno," she had said. "It's free. I'm trying it out so my students can use it when classes begin in the fall."

Katie's friendship with Carol went back to 1975, when the newly-married Krausses had just moved to Cabot. At that time they purchased a ranch-style house on Mt. Carmel Road, a quarter mile from where they now lived. Adjacent was another "ranch" with a long driveway that circled a pond. That home belonged to Carol and her husband, Sam.

At that time, Carol's daughter was two. She had a son the

following year, the same year in which Katie's Kristine was born. The women were good friends from the beginning, and their children played together.

When Carol's son was five, she discovered her husband having an affair. Many tears later, she obtained a divorce. They sold the house, and Carol and her two children moved into a smaller place on Meadowlark Street in downtown Cabot.

Fortunately, Carol had a teaching degree from the University of Connecticut. Her specialty, math, enabled her to get a job teaching high school geometry. As her children got older, she took computer courses at the University of Arkansas at Little Rock during the summer months. She now taught a computer science course part-time.

As Katie contemplated her response to Frank, she thought again about e-mailing. What if she e-mailed Frank using their America on Line (AOL) program, but cautioned him to respond via Carol's address? No, that wouldn't do. Frank would have Ken's e-mail address and might inadvertently use it sometime, with disastrous consequences for her. Besides, how could she explain such a weird arrangement to Frank?

There was only one way to correspond in e-mail. Katie had to have her own address. Maybe she could install and uninstall the Juno program each time she wanted to send an e-mail. No. Wait. Carol had told her that, while installation was simple, each time it involved a time-consuming registration procedure. Imagine going through that process every day, just to see if an e-mail was there waiting for her! Could she be sure Ken would not somehow discover her practice? And what about the Cabot-to-Little Rock telephone charges for reaching the nearest Juno modem? They'd show up on their telephone bill.

In the wee morning hours, Katie thought of a feasible plan. She'd use Carol's computer to send and receive e-mail messages with her own Juno address. She would compose the letter at home on her word processor, save it to a diskette, go to Carol's place, and open the file on the word-processor there. Then she could quickly copy the text from the screen, paste it into the Juno drafting block, and send it off as an e-mail to Frank.

Whenever Carol saw a letter from Frank in her in-box, she could call Katie, who would drive over and get it. Katie would reimburse Carol for the long-distance phone calls. That was the perfect solution.

Katie knew Carol would agree with it. She despised Ken ever since she overheard him belittle Katie one morning in the presence of a television deliveryman.

*** 

Katie and Carol were in the kitchen drinking coffee while Ken helped a deliveryman set up the television. All of a sudden Ken appeared at the kitchen door, very irritated. "Are you deaf, Kitten? How many times do I have to call you?"

"I'm sorry," Katie said meekly. "I didn't hear you call."

"Well I called you twice. Get your ass in here and help us now!"

Katie immediately got up from her chair and followed Ken.

Carol interrupted. "But I didn't...."

"Katie doesn't need you to defend her!" Ken snarled. "Go on home! As a matter of fact, I don't want to ever see you in this house again!"

Carol went home but was sorry she had not spoken up more in Katie's behalf. Later in the day she telephoned Katie.

"It's so humiliating the way Ken talks to you. I was sitting right there in the kitchen and I didn't hear him call you either. I should have stood my ground and spoken up in your behalf. Why I let him bully me into leaving so quickly is beyond me. I guess I didn't want a scene."

"It's okay, Carol. I didn't want a scene either."

"It's not right that he speaks to you like that. Believe me, I'll be more than happy to never see him again. It's like losing a wart! But I don't want to lose you as a friend. We'll still be friends, won't we?"

"Yes, and don't worry. You can come over any time you want to when Ken isn't home. And I'll come into town lots of times and see you."

"Of course, Katie, you could have spoken up in your own behalf instead of meekly following him."

"I've tried that in the past. It only makes matters worse. Some people are willing to take a dispute to any level in order to win."

"You can't even speak up in your defense when you're harmed! Katie! How do you handle that? Doesn't your blood just boil when he humiliates you in front of others?"

Katie didn't answer. What could she say? It not only made her blood boil, it wounded her heart and made her skin tighten, as if this could somehow put more space between her and Ken. She had learned a stiff drink deadened these feelings. Nevertheless, when the drinks wore off, shadows of the hurt remained.

\*\*\*

Katie returned to the letter she was holding in her hands. No doubt about it, since Frank had an e-mail address, 'e-mailing was the way to go. Besides, she wanted to appear modern, technologically savvy, to be a part of Silicon Valley.

Now that she had a way to respond to Frank, she nestled the letter once again between the two plates and went to bed. In the morning she telephoned Carol and asked her about using the Juno program.

"Oh course, no problem," said Carol. "I'll stop by and we can talk about it—if Ken won't be home, that is."

"He's gone to work and won't be home until around five-thirty."

"Good. I'm playing golf this morning with my usual summer foursome. Usual, that is, since you left us two years ago. I wish you'd come back. I miss you.

"Oh, I know, it's your limp. You hardly do anything anymore because of that. But you really could. You're not the only one in this world with a limp.

"Besides, Katie, lots of people in this world with limps don't have your looks. High cheekbones, blond tresses, hazel eyes, perfect complexion. Wow! All that and a gorgeous body too! I should hate you! But I don't, because most women with what you have are conceited. You're different—so sweet inside! That jerk, Ken, doesn't deserve you."

"But Carol, I'm envious of *you*. You have your degree."

"You could go back to school."

"I've tried several times, as you know. But it's always the same. I miss a lot of classes because Ken wants me to travel with him. I fall too far behind. Then I have to quit."

"Think about doing it again, Katie. Don't give up so easily! Well, see you. Gotta run."

After she hung up, Katie pondered over her friend's comments. She was hypersensitive about the limp. But it was painful to her emotionally. For one thing, the *way* she had gotten the limp angered her. Also, she no longer could tuck her long, slender legs into the high heels she loved to wear. Those legs, after all, had been the key to her escape from a plain world.

Carol came over after golf and ate lunch with Katie. Katie explained about Frank and her desire to e-mail. "Naturally," she said, "I can't do it here. If Ken found out, he would be livid."

Carol ran her fingers through her clove-colored curls. She twirled a few of the short fringes, then placed them around the edges of her porcelain face. Her cinnamon eyes sparkled with anticipation. "You're doing something behind Ken's back! That's so delicious! Maybe someday you'll get up the gumption to actually leave him. There's only one thing, Katie. I won't know when you've received a message. Unless you give me your password, that is. And if you do, I promise on a stack of Bibles I won't read your messages."

"I know you'd never do that," Katie replied. "Let me think of a good password. I know! 'Heron.' How's that sound?"

"Sounds good. But Katie—curiosity killed the cat, and I'm not ready to die yet—so, tell me, how did you come up with 'heron?'"

"That's what my maiden name means in German. I didn't know that until Frank mentioned it in his letter. I *love* the images it inspires, visions of a long, sleek body with neck and legs extended in graceful flight, above the trees, above the tallest buildings, soaring to freedom.... You won't forget it, will you?"

"With those descriptions, I doubt it," laughed Carol.

For the next few days Katie thought about how to answer the letter hiding between the plates. Soon Frank would leave for Germany. She *had* to get a letter to him before then. She wrote dozens of little notes, then tore them up and threw them away. She had to be professional in her response. After all, he was looking for a book partner, not a friendship. Nonetheless, they were third cousins, so a little personal information would be in order. She finally decided upon the following letter:

> *Dear Frank,*
> 
> *Thank you for your congratulations, which meant a lot to me. My given name is Katharina and I am the Katie who lived in the Columbiana area nearly thirty years ago. And yes, my family was Old Order Mennonites. We moved out of the area after my father, who had struggled bravely against leukemia, succumbed to the disease.*

> As a child, I saw the devastating symptoms of leukemia, his fatigue, his paleness. We called it "white blood." I could not have possibly known as a child that meant his red cell count was low, his blood flooded with white cells, and his immune system jeopardized.
>
> When I returned home from school one day with a fever and rash, I saw a worried look flash across my mother's face. The next thing I knew, someone posted a "Quarantine!" sign on our house. Such ugly red letters. No one could come in; no one was to leave. But my father left. He left in a box. He came down with a fever and rash—the scarlet fever I had brought into the house. The disease overwhelmed his already weakened body.

Katie related the story about her father's struggle to farm: "I found him lying on the ground in the cornfield and gave him lemonade. He asked me not to tell Mama where I had found him. His words were full of hope, and he assured me his red blood was coming back. I should have told my mother."

A few years after his death, the family moved away from the Columbiana area. The letter continued:

> It's funny how it all came about, the move that is. My mother was shopping in Columbiana one day. She went to town as an Old Order Mennonite; she came home as someone else.
>
> Some followers of Kathryn Kuhlman were handing out tracts. They gave Mama one. It was all about faith-healing. Mama was flabbergasted. She wondered why, in her religion, people did not pray for the sick by the laying on of hands as had been done in the early church. Maybe Papa could have been healed! she exclaimed for weeks.
>
> The tract listed the time and station number of a radio show where Kathryn could be heard. Mama, whose religion forbade radios, now went out and bought one. She

*faithfully tuned to Ms. Kuhlman. So captured by a religion that believed in healing, within six months Mama renounced her Old Order membership, sold the farm and moved our entire family to Pittsburgh so that she could follow Kathryn Kuhlman's religion.*

*The move from the Old Order community made a tremendous difference in my life. As one of the younger children, I was allowed to go on to high school and graduate. Unfortunately—and it saddens me to think about this—my oldest brothers and sisters had to quit school after the eighth grade because of Mennonite rules.*

*It seems so strange to think back on all this now, but I was actually afraid to move away from the farm, afraid that if I did not have Papa's memories around me, I would forget him.*

*I learned, however, that memories are not tied to one location; they go wherever you go. When I moved to Pittsburgh, my father moved with me; when I moved to Cabot, he came here too. To this day he is alive within me.*

*Whenever I see someone tall and lean with a full head of dark, straight hair, I see my father and my heart leaps. Whenever I hear soft-spoken speech, shivers run up and down my back. Whenever I feel a weak hand in mine, a hand without structure, I feel his hand as we walked from the cornfield. And whenever I see a coffin, I cry as I remember the box that left our house that late fall afternoon, a body beaten by scarlet fever.*

*Frank, your letter was such a pleasant surprise for it brought memories of my father back to me. I think it was how you phrased your words, your approach, that kindness and tenderness in your written words that reminded me of my father's approach. It bathed me in warmth and sent me back to my childhood days.*

*I'm glad you are going with your mother to Germany. Is your father still living? I had no idea about this Johann* fellow. I thought my great-great-grandfather was named John. Could you please give me more information about all this, maybe e-mail me a chart or something so that I can see exactly how you and I are related?

I have written quite a few short stories and poems, but have not attempted anything as large as a book. At first the idea frightened me, but, as I got to thinking about it, realized that a book is just a lot of short stories. Now it no longer seems insurmountable. Besides, I like challenge. So I definitely will think about collaborating on a book with you.

You can correspond with me at the following e-mail address: krkrauss@Juno.com. I log on at my girlfriend Carol's house. It is very important that you do not mail letters or telephone me at my home. I hope you'll understand.
Sincerely,
Katie
PS: I hope you and your mother have a wonderful trip in Germany. Please write and tell me all about it when you get back.

# 3

## PLEIDELSHEIM

Frank checked his mailbox every day. No letter arrived from Katie. Only a week had passed. He should allow her more time to respond, but doubts began to plague him. Did she think he was a crank? A dreamer unable to recognize the limitations of his talent?

Why should she, a prestigious award winner, want to collaborate on a book with him? How could she be *sure* he was the relative he said he was? Frank shuddered as he thought of cases in which perverts pursued famous women. He should have sent Katie the descendants' chart. Of that he was now sure.

His fertile mind found other, less troublesome reasons for her not having responded. Maybe she hadn't even received his letter. Frank recalled a telephone bill he had once paid that was returned weeks later in the Postal Service equivalent to a body bag: totally mangled in the machinery for sorting letters, with only his return address still visible. Maybe Katie wasn't even home. She could be on an extended vacation with her husband.

In his heart of hearts, Frank knew his stress was caused by his silly desire to receive an answer before his trip to Germany. "What difference would it make if she delayed her response?" he asked in a cross-examination of himself. "What difference if she didn't respond at all! Would he collect more information in Germany if he knew she would collaborate with him on a book? Of course not." He intended to write a book, regardless of Katie's decision. Why, then, his great concern that she answer his letter before he left?

Intellectually, he couldn't understand this desire. It didn't make sense. Two weeks ago he hadn't even known of a Katie Reyher Krauss. Emotionally, however, he felt as uneasy leaving without a letter from Katie as he would have felt leaving his toothbrush behind.

He buried himself in his genealogy work, then went online to see if he had received any responses to the invitation on his homepage for genealogical information. Mail in the inbox! What's this? Mail? It was more like a bombshell—a letter from "krkrauss@Juno.com"!

What a surprise! In all of his musings, it had never occurred to him that Katie might respond by e-mail.

Frank's hands turned clammy, like those of an unprepared student just starting a final exam. "Settle down," he scolded himself. "Read the message first!" Maybe she wasn't the Katie he was looking for. Maybe she didn't want to collaborate on a book. Maybe this. Maybe that.

He clicked her e-mail onto the screen and read, completely absorbed. An earthquake could not have distracted him.

By the time he finished, Frank was a bundle of emotions. He got up from his chair and walked around the room. "It's as if she knows me."

He went to the window, opened it, and took deep breaths of the refreshing spring air. He watched as two robins sang love songs to each other, then bobbed from tree to tree with bits of nesting material secured between their beaks. His eyes caught the recently-opened colorful blossoms of columbines; their finest stamens projected outward. Several honeybees tasted their sweet nectar, their feet yellowed with pollen.

Children rode their bikes up and down the street, their laughter filling the air. Frank felt as fresh as a bear emerging from a long, dark winter of hibernation, and taking a roll in a bed of spring beauties.

How easy it was to connect with her! She *knew* what it was like to fear moving because of memories left behind. Just like him. He avoided selling his house because of Sally's clothes in the closet, her perfume in the bathroom—everything left as it had been the day she died. Throwing anything out meant somehow throwing *her* out as well. Hadn't he disappointed her enough already? That awful emergency room scene.

Katie was right. How had she put it? That memories were not tied to one location. Triggering stimuli surrounded people no matter where they were. Cataracts fell from Frank's eyes, enabling him to see the obvious. Of course! He was the carrier of Sally's wonderful memories, and wherever he went, Sally would be.

"Maybe I can finally get on with my life." Frank relaxed and brushed back a disobedient lock of hair.

He returned to his computer, where the screen saver exploded with fireworks. He hit a key and her letter came back into view.

He rubbed his chin as he reread the e-mail, then closed his eyes to think. She seems to feel guilty about her father's death. Just as I feel guilty about Dad's death. I noticed him stumble. Yet I said nothing. If only I had insisted he be tested, he might still be alive today.

Frank wondered if all this was meant to be. Was their collaboration "written in the Great Book," as he had heard Muslims express it? If so, why had fate singled them out for such an honor?

But there was a more perplexing question. Why had she used her girlfriend's Juno program? Didn't she have e-mail capability at home? And why had she ruled out telephone calls or regular mail? It seemed more like a warning. That seemed odd. Oh, well, he thought, whatever her reasons, they wouldn't affect their proposed book collaboration. When Katie wanted to tell him more, she would. Nevertheless, the stuff "unsaid" left him with an inexplicable sense of being needed.

Should he mention Sally in his response? No, that meant a baring of his soul, a nakedness for which he was not yet ready. And guilt so raw, blood would surely drip from his typing fingers. He'd share the "tamer" story, the one about his father.

He copied and saved the e-mail under *Personal*, then wondered why he hadn't filed it under one of his professional folders. But to do so seemed like placing a rose in a field of soybeans. He exited his e-mail program and turned off the computer.

He'd put off a response for now. Attaching a descendants' chart would be easy. But composing a well-thought-out response was not. He must get it right. Besides, in waiting until after his return, he hoped he would have a lot more to tell her about their illustrious common ancestry.

Frank was in unusually high spirits as he prepared for his trip. Finally, the day of departure arrived. His suitcase was packed. Before he left the house, however, he printed a copy of Katie's letter and placed it among his important papers. It made sense, he reasoned, to have the letter with him. After all, he had to keep her interests in mind. She was not only his collaborator, but also his third cousin. Anything he and his mother discovered on their genealogical quest belonged to Katie as well.

A few weeks later Frank returned home. The usual dull feeling he encountered when first stepping inside the door was gone, replaced by exhilaration and anticipation. His thoughts were on Katie and he couldn't wait to share his fantastic trip to Germany with her.

He glanced at the stack of mail awaiting him, sorted the bills, and set them aside. He watered plants and hacked away at his swollen pile of dirty laundry. At last he was ready. Tomorrow he'd return to work, but tonight belonged to Katie.

In preparation, he carefully placed the printed copy of Katie's letter in front of him. Countless unfolding, reading and refolding, had given it the bedraggled look of a washed dollar bill. He sat at his computer and began his response.

*Dear Katie,*

*I wanted to wait until my return from Germany before answering your e-mail so that I could tell you a lot more about our ancestors. The wait was worth it in that respect, although I have to admit, there were many times I found it hard not sending you cards and air-mail letters.*

*Your e-mail delighted me both literally and figuratively. Literally, because it removed my last lingering doubts over whether I had found the right Reyher. Figuratively, because it brought me joy to discover a woman with a refreshing directness and an ability to touch others' souls with real-life stories. No wonder you won the Faulkner prize!*

*Your story about your family, and especially the memories of your father, meant much to me. I was amazed to learn that my first letter had somehow helped to reawaken these memories. Losing him when he contracted scarlet fever must have been horrible for you, especially since you were so young. I know you feel a certain amount of guilt about all this. But you must realize you are not to blame. It is not up to a little girl of eight to know about compromised immune systems. You can take heart in knowing your father's remarkable, indomitable spirit in his struggle against leukemia.*

*I know how it is with guilt, however. You can't get rid of it because someone says you shouldn't feel it. My own* father, when seventy-one, suffered a massive stroke. It turned him into a shell of his former self. He lived that way for six months, then died. I had seen him stumble a few days earlier. He had laughed about it, and said, "My mother always told me to pick up my feet. Will I ever learn?"

I realized too late that Dad's little joke about his misstep was an attempt on his part to save face. His stumble was a warning. I should have known that! (It's strange to be telling you this story. I never mentioned it to anyone before.)

Over the past few weeks I have been ruminating endlessly over the importance of fate as opposed to chance in our lives. Was it fate, for instance, that brought us in contact right now? I find it odd that the announcement of your award came out in the Columbiana paper only a couple of weeks before my planned trip to Germany. Were our paths predestined to cross? Or was it pure chance—a simple toss of the die—with our number just happening to come up?

I see both fate and chance as having time, space and readiness dimensions, and I find it interesting how these three dimensions come together when paths cross. Let me explain.

For instance, at the TIME of your award announcement that appeared in my SPACE, I was into genealogy and READY to do something with the information.

These dimensions apply to you also, but in a different way. I am sure you worked for years (TIME) to develop your writing to the point where it was possible to win such an award (which could be considered a legal entity in SPACE). Now, you possess the skills, which makes you READY (I hope so anyway), to join me in writing a book.

The great-great-grandfather whom you call John is actually Johann Gotthard Reyher. We share his fantastic heritage. Johann married a girl named Katharina Wilhelm. Am I right in assuming that you were named after her?

It may interest you to know that the farm Johann bought after marrying Katharina had belonged to her father, Elias Friedrich "Frederick" Wilhelm. It was in Beaver Township. I was wondering exactly where you lived in Columbiana.

But enough of all that. What I really want to do is share with you my wonderful trip. My mother and I experienced a most breathtaking walk back into the lives of our ancestors. The stories we uncovered now course through my veins. My hope is to convey some of this excitement to you.

First, a little history about how I learned so much of our background. When a good friend of mine got me started in genealogy, my mother gave me an envelope labeled "genealogy stuff." It had come down through the family to my grandmother, who had meticulously added many further names to it. When she died, the envelope was turned over to my mother. I had your name as well as those of your brothers and sisters because my grandmother had regularly perused the birth announcements appearing in the Columbiana paper.

Information contained in this envelope told us that Johann Gotthard Reyher, born in 1798, had entered America in 1819 through the port of Philadelphia. This whetted our appetite—OUR, because by this time my mother had become very interested in our heritage as well. She actually started the processes that resulted in our discovery of Pleidelsheim, the Reyhers' ancestral home. But I'm getting ahead of myself.

Mom's genealogical groundwork revealed that Johann Gotthard had come to the New World by ship from Amsterdam. Family records showed he was German, and library research indicated that most Germans departed for the New World through Amsterdam. But where had Johann lived in Germany? And was that within today's Germany? He could have come from German-inhabited areas in other European countries, such as Alsace in France.

As our search for Johann's hometown continued, we received two big clues. The first came during a visit to my great-uncle, Isaac Reyher, then a still very lucid 100-year-old. Knowing of my ties to Germany as an exchange student long ago, he said, seemingly out of the blue, "It must be beautiful along the Neckar in Tshermany." (He couldn't pronounce a soft "g" properly.) It was obvious that this was not a fleeting statement, but a kind of sign from deep within his memories, perhaps stemming from nostalgic stories told by his grandfather, Johann Gotthard.

The second clue emerged during an intense search of the Reyhers' legal documents. Among them we discovered a will—probated in the U.S. but written in the old German script (virtually illegible these days for younger-generation Germans)—made by Johann Gotthard's father, Johann Melchior Reyher, in the United States!

We now knew that Johann Melchior–incidentally, our great-great-great-grandfather—had also emigrated. He and his wife Anna had joined their son in the U.S. in 1834. Fifteen years after Johann Gotthard had left them behind in Germany!

I find it amazing that two older people like that could leave family, friends, cherished land, everything behind and come to America for a new life. Think how difficult travel was in those days!

To go on with the story, a classmate from one of my German courses helped me translate the will, and we learned that Johann Melchior's assets in the old country had been in a place ending in "heim" under the jurisdiction of a town called Marbach a.N.

There are a number of Marbachs in Germany, but I figured that "a.N.," a typical abbreviation, probably stood for "am [on the] Neckar," which certainly was consistent with the "sign" Uncle Isaac had given me.

Mom and I had this information in hand as we left for Germany, and decided we would start our search in Marbach am Neckar.

We flew USAir out of Pittsburgh. As is typical of Europe-bound flights, we arrived in Frankfurt in the early morning hours. By rental car we drove straight to Marbach a.N., a trip that these days takes less than two hours by autobahn. Jet lag means nothing when you're keyed up, so we went straight to the church office in Marbach.

We were lucky in one way. A secretary was there to help us who had time to spare and a knowledge of the old German script. But she failed to find any references to our family of Reyhers in the meticulously-kept church records on births, baptisms, marriages, and deaths. Jet lag suddenly caught up with us and we felt very weary.

We thanked the lady, contributed generously to the church's restoration fund, and started to leave when she suddenly said, "Wait a minute, I have an idea. In those days Marbach was a regional headquarters. There were many outlying churches under its jurisdiction. Maybe one of them was where your ancestors came from."

She looked through her files and found a list for Marbach district. It contained twenty-six towns, many of them with several churches. Mom and I looked at each other and groaned. Even if we had the time—which we didn't—the thought of possibly having to visit that many churches was a total downer.

Then it was my turn to have an idea. "How many of

these places end in 'heim?'" I asked. We counted five—a universe considerably more doable than twenty-six!

"Of course," I said cautiously, "the Reyhers could have lived in other places ending in 'heim' but without a church. Villages around here are so close together they might have had just a fifteen-minute walk or buggy ride to get to a nearby church." However, when I saw despair in Mom's eyes, I decided to add, "But at least we can get started with the ones we know about."

No one contradicted my logic. Anyway, we agreed, the haystack had become smaller, making it easier to find the needle. It was a challenge we both relished. We had not come this far to give up now. So, after a night of tending to our jet lag, we started our search.

Day 1: Hoepfigheim, Mundelsheim. No luck.

Day 2: Ottmarsheim, Steinheim. Again no luck.

Day 3: Pleidelsheim. "Come back in the morning," we were told. "The secretary is not here this afternoon."

Thus, just as we were about to lose the courage of our conviction, we struck gold. The next morning in Pleidelsheim a friendly church secretary, Frau Wolf, found the answer to our quest. The Reyhers' ancestral home was in Pleidelsheim am Neckar. Frau Wolf provided all the information on our family we had sought, and more.

To our amazement, the records showed that the Reyhers had not lived in Pleidelsheim throughout recorded time, but that the dynasty there had actually begun when a Hans Reyher came from Ruswil, a little place in Switzerland, in 1654 to claim a homestead. This was shortly after the Thirty Years' War. Imagine! Our genealogy quest that had brought us to Pleidelsheim suddenly catapulted us back another one-hundred-fifty years! Mom and I couldn't have been more excited, and the church restoration fund there benefited accordingly.

We wanted to experience and explore Johann's town,

which now had become Hans' town as well, so we set about finding a place to stay. Katie, you wouldn't believe the great time we had! It's not Heidelberg or Rothenburg, but it's charming and it's our town! You'd love Pleidelsheim!

We checked into the comfortable new Hotel Ochsen (which, as you might have guessed, means "oxen"). Talk about fate! It turns out that the hotel incorporates an inn or restaurant by the same name that already existed when Hans Reyher arrived in Pleidelsheim some three-hundred-forty years ago! And that Hans' only surviving child, Johann Caspar, who himself ran an inn called "Stern" (which means "star" and which continued to exist until 1953), had married the daughter of the Ochsen proprietor. (I'm ahead of myself, but all this will fit into place if we do the book together.) So that was how Mom and I came to eat in a restaurant that had belonged to another of our ancestors!

Anyhow, we decided to walk around as much as Mom was able—which, incidentally, was a lot more than I expected. The place seemed to be a tonic for her.

At the suggestion of the proprietor, we first visited the modern Rathaus, or town hall. On a hunch, I asked to see the burgermeister (mayor). Upon learning we were American, his assistant quickly ushered us into his office.

The burgermeister, a youngish man named Erwin Paulus, was obviously delighted to see us. In fact, when he heard why we were in Pleidelsheim, he dropped a bombshell. "Have you seen the beautiful half-timbered house on Torgasse that your ancestor, Johann Melchior Reyher, built in 1798?"

Mom and I looked at each other, our eyes reflecting our astonishment. We were both thinking, "Built in 1798? That's the year of Johann Gotthard's birth."

The perplexed looks on our faces prompted Paulus to

*explain how he came across that information.* "Remember, Pleidelsheim is not a big town. Anyhow, a few years back as I was trying to create some enthusiasm for restoration projects, I worked on a number of houses myself. It just happened that I was the one who, while hacking stucco away from the facade of Torgasse 2, found the long-hidden Reyher sign. I'll take you there," he said. "Nothing in the old section of town is very far away from this office."

He had his secretary give us a simple map and some informational materials on the town. Included was a small picture book, "Pleidelsheim, Pictures from Days Past," with a drawing of the town as it appeared in 1682. We found this particularly interesting, knowing that Hans Reyher was a resident there at the time.

We set off to visit this home from our past, at Torgasse 2, which turned out indeed to be only a little over a block away. Paulus explained that the town had recently celebrated twelve-hundred years of documented existence. "Pleidelsheim is actually much older, though," he said. "There are even signs of Roman settlement here."

We walked down Mundelsheimer Strasse to the start of Hauptstrasse (Main Street). There, in the middle of the intersection (as can only happen in Europe), was the old Rathaus, handsomely restored. A sign indicated it had been built in 1614. "Just think, Mom," I said, "this is probably where Hans Reyher first went in 1654 to claim his homestead."

"Almost certainly," Paulus agreed. "Actually, quite a few immigrants ended up in Pleidelsheim after the Thirty Years' War," he added helpfully. "They were needed. The town had lost ninety percent of its population to war and the plague."

After walking about a block down Haupstrasse (which, incidentally, we later learned was called Gross-Ingersheimer Str. in the 19th century, Ingersheim being the village to which the street led), we arrived at the side street called Torgasse. There, to our left, with the address of Torgasse 2, was the beautiful half-timbered Reyher house.

"This is a very historical spot," Paulus said. "The whole complex, including the court behind this arched doorway in the wall, is called the Hasenhof." (FYI, Katie: 'hof' means 'farm' in this context). Paulus continued, "It was named after one of my predecessors, Joerg Haas, who, along with various family members, lived here when he took office in 1574. So your ancestor Johann Melchior Reyher built on a prestigious site."

Paulus took his leave to return to his office, leaving us to gawk at the house. We noted the inscription high up on one of the corner timbers: "Built by Johann Melchior Reyher in 1798." We were admiring the flower boxes below the windows filled with red geraniums, a typical embellishment of German houses, when suddenly one of the windows opened. An elderly lady looked down at us and said, "Would you like a look inside?"

We were embarrassed, realizing that we must have appeared to be snooping. "No, thank you, Ma'am," I uttered in my most obsequious German. "Please forgive us for staring at your house. We're just interested because our ancestor built it."

The lady appeared in no way offended. "So that's it," she said. "I knew you must have a special interest in this house when I happened to see Burgermeister Paulus pointing it out to you. My name is Frau Rupprecht. Please come in and take a look."

Mom and I were delighted to accept. After we had introduced ourselves, Frau Rupprecht showed us around.

The house was a fascinating mixture of the old and new. We could see from the supporting beams, mostly exposed and in their natural color, how well it had been built. The floors were modern, the kitchen well-equipped, and everything extremely tastefully executed. In short, it was a home that would have pleased the Reyher family.

Frau Rupprecht offered us a cup of coffee, but, knowing how Germans were given to such pro forma gestures, I said, "Thanks so much, but we really have to be on our way."

We said good-bye, and Mom and I followed Torgasse around past a section of the old town wall and back to Hauptstrasse. Everywhere were carefully tended gardens in which we could admire poppies, hyacinths, peonies and many European flowers we didn't recognize. We had seen the church tower and, since it was only a half-block away, decided to backtrack to get there.

The Mauritius (Lutheran) church is a Romanesque little gem built between 1250 and 1350. Imagine, Katie! The church had already been there for at least three hundred years when Hans Reyher arrived in Pleidelsheim from Switzerland! The nearby parsonage, by contrast, was "new," built in 1783.

Unfortunately, as is normal these days in Germany, the church was locked and we could only see the outside. Nevertheless, we were impressed.

We decided to keep exploring. Practically right next to the church, on Hauptstrasse, was another beautiful half-timbered building: The Old School House. One of our brochures indicated that it had been built in 1698 by a Johann David Oehler, who in one person embodied the school principal, court recorder, surveyor and church organist. A Renaissance man, who perhaps once taught the son and grandchildren of Hans Reyher!

We walked down Hauptstrasse until we had a good view of the river. We found nothing particularly quaint there, since there was a new bridge for auto traffic toward Ingersheim and a sewage disposal plant. In the distance we could see the woods, consisting mainly of spruce and oak, *as we were later told at the hotel. Because of the size of the trees, we conjectured that some of them must have already been there during Johann Gotthard's childhood.*

*We regretted not being able to see the old covered bridge, which had been washed out by the flooding Neckar in 1946. It occurred to us, though, that maybe the same sort of flood conditions had greeted Hans Reyher in the early spring of 1654 when he presumably came up the Neckar.*

*We decided to return to the hotel. Even I was bushed, so you can imagine how my elderly mother must have felt. But we were also in a great mood.*

*It was time to spoil ourselves with a good dinner, so we went to the Ochsen restaurant, where we were treated like visiting royalty (especially after they learned of our discoveries that day!). We mentioned wanting to sample a local wine—we recalled from the informational brochure that, until modern times, wine-making had been just as important as farming to the economy of Pleidelsheim— and the Ochsen insisted on serving us a bottle of their best Trollinger on the house. It was a light, dry red wine, which we were informed had been a favorite local variety for hundreds of years.*

*The next morning, we walked around the town some more, past Torgasse 2 again, but also into other parts of the old section of town that we had not yet seen. It was sunny and unseasonably warm—after a cold spring, we were told— and the cherry and apple trees were now in full bloom.*

*No doubt about it, Pleidelsheim was an attractive place. We began to wonder why the Reyhers had left it. Obviously, they had not been poor. From our research before our trip, we were pretty sure why Johann Gotthard left Germany, but why had his parents done so too at the ages of fifty-nine and fifty-seven? As Mom and I strolled the streets of Pleidelsheim, we went over what we thought might be the main reasons.*

While the Reyhers might have been relatively wealthy, there was no social net in those days. Consequently, no one's economic fate was far removed from potential disaster. I recalled from my pre-trip reading that in 1816 (just three years before Johann Gotthard's emigration), there had been a disastrous harvest in the Kingdom of Wuerttemberg. With land limited—most farmers owned between twenty and thirty acres—there was never much chance to build up significant reserves. The U.S., with its standard quarter section (160 acres) available for practically nothing, must have looked pretty attractive by comparison. Besides, it was normal for parents to look to their oldest son for support in old age.

Perhaps more importantly, as I learned from subsequent reading, Pleidelsheim, while itself a reasonably well-governed town, had, over the centuries, repeatedly been a victim of machinations and failings of other political jurisdictions, including what by 1806 had come to be called the Kingdom of Wuerrtemberg.

True, with the end of the Napoleonic wars a period of peace had set in, and, with a new constitution promulgated in 1819, absolutism in Wuerttemberg was finally dead. But, as you will eventually see if we do a book together, there were still good reasons to find fault with the policies of the Kingdom of which the Reyhers were subjects. (Remember what I wrote in my first letter about a draft of young men for mercenary duty.) In that context, America—about which Europe then as now was quite well informed—must have looked pretty attractive, despite its wild west reputation.

So there it is, Katie, your introduction to Pleidelsheim and how we discovered it. It's so exhilarating to uncover genealogical roots and the stories that go with them. Naturally, everyone's story is different, but I think you'll have to agree that we have particularly interesting ones to tell. Don't you think there is drama there? I am sure you, as an experienced writer, can spin some great yarns set in the context I have sketched. How about it?

I am wondering if you ever get back to Columbiana. I live on the south side of Youngstown. It would be an easy shot there from my home. I would love to meet you sometime.
With warm regards,
Frank.
PS: I am attaching the descendants' chart you requested.

# 4

## CHINESE ACROBATS

The telephone rang. "Hey, Katie," said Carol. "You have an e-mail from Frank."

"Oh, wonderful. That means he's back from his trip. I'll come over now and get it, if you're going to be home."

"I'll be home. Say, how about Pizza Hut for lunch?"

"Sounds good to me. I'll retrieve the letter. Then we'll go for lunch."

A short time later Katie clicked into Carol's Juno program. She entered her password, highlighted Frank's message, and watched it come onto the screen.

"Wow! It's lo-o-ong," said Katie to her friend. "I'll print it out and read it later."

The message printed page after page.

"What's he doing, writing you a book?" asked Carol.

"I don't know," laughed Katie. "It looks like it, doesn't it?"

"Well, Katie, you're going to have to buy me toner and paper if this continues," teased Carol. "But, naturally, I don't care. I just like to see you happy. And this guy makes you happy, doesn't he? It's refreshing to see you laugh this way. Now this is the kind of laughter I like to see. Not that fake laughter you produce for Ken."

"You don't have to keep bringing that up," said Katie, a little annoyed.

"I can't help it. It makes me sick." To emphasize the point, Carol pointed her finger into her open mouth toward her throat and made a couple of gagging sounds.

"Let's just call it a survival technique," Katie said in her defense. "It's nothing unusual. Look at the employee who laughs at his boss's jokes even after being tongue-lashed in front of others. Or at the child who is repeatedly berated by a parent. Doesn't he laugh again in the presence of his parents? No one, in fact, can tell the difference between the harmed and the unharmed when it comes to laughter in the presence of the abuser."

"You call it a survival technique! I call it groveling behavior. It reminds me of a dog who has just been whipped by his master, then crawls back on his belly at his master's command."

However, for fear of upsetting Katie, Carol changed the subject. "Let's get back to this Frank guy. What do you know about him?"

"He's my cousin. Other than that, I don't know much about him. He just wants to write a book with me."

"How old is he? Is he married?"

"I don't know the answer to either of those questions. It isn't important. He took a trip to Germany with his mother so they could look up genealogy stuff."

"Not with his wife? That suggests he's not married. A foreign trip is special. No wife would miss out on a trip to Germany, even if her mother-in-law were along. He's definitely not married. So, see there. Ha! I have one of my questions answered just like that!" exclaimed Carol as she snapped her fingers.

Carol resumed her interrogation, "What does he do for a living?"

"Please. Enough! I've only had one letter from him. Before this one, that is. How am I supposed to know all these things from one letter?"

"I would!"

"Oh, I know *you* would," laughed Katie.

"Well, after you read all those pages and if you still don't have a clue as to whether he is married, how old he is, or what he does, just ask me to write the next letter."

"Never!" Katie laughed, but inside she felt her heart lurch. Sharing Frank with Carol in this way would have been like being required, as a child, to share a newly-discovered four-leaf clover with a friend.

"It's eleven-thirty," said Carol. "Are you ready for lunch?"

"Sure. Let's go."

"I'll be leaving directly from Pizza Hut for Little Rock, so we'd better both drive."

"Meeting Paul again, are you?"

Carol smiled conspiratorially, and soon the two of them were entering the front door of Pizza Hut and sliding into a table by the door. Silently, but gratefully, Katie acknowledged Carol's compassion. Her friend knew how embarrassing she found it to limp across dining rooms.

"I'm famished," said the rather plump Carol. "I've eaten hardly anything all week."

"Starving yourself again to lose a few pounds for Paul?" Katie teased.

"Actually, I don't do it for Paul. I do it for myself. I pluck the strings on my violin and am responsible for my own happiness. I no longer dance to someone else's tune." She gave Katie a *like you* glance, then added, "See how much I've grown up over the years?"

Sensing her glance might have offended Katie, she changed the subject. "Okay if I order our usual? A medium supreme pan, iced teas?"

"Sure, that's fine," said Katie. "What time do you meet Paul?"

"He gets out at two, but I need to leave by one at the latest. It takes about an hour to drive to Little Rock."

"What's he taking this summer?"

"Biology. Always biology. It's the only way a teacher of life sciences can keep up with that exploding field of knowledge."

"When are you two getting married? You've been seeing each other for . . . how long has it been now?"

"Five years. Would you believe it!"

"It's a long time to go together and not get married. I see the sparkle in your eyes, the lift of your step, the bounce of your hair as you walk, all telltale signs of a person in love."

"I do love him. But getting burned once makes a person very cautious around stoves. I'm certainly in no hurry to get married again."

"I can understand your reluctance."

The iced teas arrived. Katie took a Valium from her purse and washed it down with the cool liquid.

"See, there you go again. Ever since I've known you, you've been on those pills. When in the world did you start?"

"Shortly after I got married."

"I should have known it had something to do with that jerk, Ken. But after all these years, Katie, you've got to stop! They're not intended to be taken long-term. Why don't you see a counselor?"

"Sometimes words are so deeply submerged, it's hard to get them into your mouth. What good would it do to see a counselor when I can't verbalize what's wrong?"

"Why don't you try it with me, Katie? Tell me exactly how you feel."

"Feel. Well, this might shock you."

"I'm not easily shocked."

"I feel as though I'm under a huge hand, Ken's hand. I'm allowed to walk around the edges, but if I venture too far, criticisms, belittlings, beratings and scoffs come at me like arrows. The injuries damage my confidence, and I become a child and scamper back under the protection of his huge hand."

"That's a shocking scene, Katie. And sickening as well.

# FLIGHTS OF THE HERONS

But very perceptive. You've been doing some serious thinking of late."

"As you know, I don't do much outside the home anymore. The only good thing I can say about my limp is that it has given me the solitude I need to write. And out of my writing comes introspection. I know that Ken is the one with the problem, not me. He is a parasite and feeds on my self-esteem at my expense. He must lower me in order to elevate himself."

Carol sat quietly as Katie continued: "Or is it that he has a huge ego, which, like a slow-leaking balloon, constantly needs to be inflated?

"The truth of the matter is, I don't really know him. He never opens himself up to me or any one else. It's as if he has encased himself in an armor of steel and is extremely afraid of exposure. And that takes me back to the same question. Is his self-encasement to protect a huge ego or a fragile one?

"Since I realized what is actually happening, however, my spirit demands freedom. The arrows still fly when I crawl out from under that awful hand, but I now stand up, strengthened by enlightenment. I've even turned my feet in an opposite direction and am marching down a path of no return."

"What I don't understand," Carol said, "is why you care whether his ego is big or fragile."

"I wouldn't want to destroy him if he has a fragile ego."

"Are you nuts? He's willing to destroy you. He puts his life ahead of yours. You exist for his consumption, whether his ego is big or little."

Carol looked at her watch. "Well, I must run. I'll get you the name of a good counselor. Say exactly what you said to me. They'll know what you're talking about.

"But, on the other hand, Katie, why should you see a counselor? *You*'re not the one who needs one. And I'll bet you ten-thousand dollars you'll never get Ken to one. So why should I go through all that bother to get you a name?"

"You shouldn't bother," Katie agreed, with a sigh. "Ken would never go to a counselor, seeing that he opens up to no one."

Her face brightened as she looked across the table at her friend, "Thanks for helping me get the words into my mouth, Carol. Things become so much clearer when you verbalize them with a good friend. Have a good time with Paul."

The friends hugged as they bid each other good-bye. "Call me tomorrow morning," said Carol, as she got into her car. "Then you can tell me all about this Frank guy."

"I will," said Katie. The thought of Frank's letter still unread made her hurry home.

Katie sat at the kitchen table and read Frank's letter. When she finished, a warmth cascaded throughout her entire body, like sweet hot chocolate after a hike on a cold winter day.

"Look at the way he treats his mother," she said to herself. "He's so compassionate, so caring! He probably treats his wife that way as well."

Oh, but did he have a wife? Katie remembered what Carol had said about going to Germany with his mother, and how no wife would let her husband spend so much precious vacation time with his mother.

Of course, the descendants' chart! That would show whether he was married and how old he was as well. Katie found his name and saw that he was fifty-six years old. And married to a Sally Angstrom. But wait! There was also a date of death after her name. She had died less than two years ago. Katie's jaw dropped. Poor Frank.

Did he have any children? Yes, two. And grandchildren as well. Katie was sure Frank had not remarried. He appeared too precise not to have entered a new wife's name. He was probably dating someone though.

Nothing there about his occupation, Katie noted. Having

been to college, he was undoubtedly a professional man of some sort.

Did she ever go to Columbiana? Frank had asked. He wanted to meet her! Katie longed to meet him too, but *not* with her limp. Why couldn't their paths have crossed two years ago? She wouldn't have hesitated for one moment then.

But, of course, there was no way she could have met him two years ago. She wasn't a famous writer then. Life played cruel games at times. Her limp had caused her to become an accomplished writer. But now she didn't want to meet people or go out of her house.

Frank was right about the intersection of three dimensions. For paths to cross, time, space and readiness all had to come together at the same time. But their paths would not cross because *she* was not ready! Or had their paths already crossed in a way? They had not met in person, of course, but readiness peeked through their communications? Katie sighed. Life could be excessively complicated at times.

Where had she lived in Columbiana? he had asked. She would tell him the whole story: that she had been born on a farm that faced Old Salem Road, the same farm as her father, and his father, grandfather and great-grandfather, who was John. Johann, as Frank called him. Imagine! She had been born on Johann's farm. "Wait 'til Frank hears this!"

She wished she had known all this when she lived in the farmhouse. She would have run her hands along the oak railing above the steps leading to the upstairs bedrooms, knowing Johann's warm hands once grasped these same railings. She would have licked off the frost on the dining room window, peered through the hole, and imagined Johann walking to the barn on a cold winter morning. So much living she could have done in her head—if only she had known about this ancestor's having come from Germany and lived in the same house as she had as a girl!

More pictures of the farmhouse flashed into her brain until

she, a girl of eleven, was sleeping in the upstairs bedroom she shared with her sisters.

***

"Time to get up, children!" called Mama. "The early bird catches the worm." Her familiar morning words ascended the hard wooden stairs, paused for a moment outside Katie's bedroom door, and then, upon finding the door ajar, hitchhiked a ride on waves already en route to exposed, sleepy ears.

There was obvious irony in Mama's words. Katie's older brothers and sisters would have long caught any available worms, for they had been up for hours doing chores on the farm or making breakfast in the kitchen. Only the younger children had the luxury of sleeping in, for they would have been more trouble than help at this busy morning hour.

Katie rubbed her sleepy eyes. Suddenly, a stage filled with prancing Chinese acrobats dressed in ballooning silks of brilliant reds, yellows, and greens flashed across her brain. The scene should have elated her; instead, it distressed her.

A school assembly. She groaned as she thought about the note she would need. Mama would write: "Sorry, but Katie is not allowed to attend the assembly because it is against our religion. Please excuse her."

Katie didn't care if she missed the assembly since she had never attended one. What did she know about them anyway, other than what the posters showed. She was tormented with the knowledge she could no longer seek refuge in the girl's bathroom. For she now knew that place was not a safe hide-out for a young girl.

Why should she have to find a place to hide while her classmates attended the assembly? Because Katie found it humiliating to remain behind. If she was in the bathroom, no one would notice she wasn't with them. This substitute activity allowed her to avoid the embarrassment of being different.

# FLIGHTS OF THE HERONS

Katie thought she had an infallible plan. When the time for assembly neared, she asked her teacher if she could go to the bathroom. Then, when she was sure that enough time had elapsed, she returned to the solitude of her classroom. It was a beautiful setup and worked perfectly, until last time ...

Hungry stomach pains replaced assembly concerns as fried ham, gravy and biscuits' aromas flooded her bedroom. She quickly exchanged her homemade nightgown for an old cotton around-the-house dress. The sun had stolen the few colors it once had, leaving only hints of a blue-checked gingham.

She joined her brothers and sisters at the table. At first there was little conversation as mouths filled with food left little space for words. Satiated stomachs slowly relinquished their monopoly over throat passages, and sentences replaced sounds of "ymmm" and "hmmm."

Or questions. Like Rebecca's. "Did Mama write you an excuse for this morning's assembly yet?"

"Not yet," said Katie.

"She already wrote me one. You'll need one too."

Visions of colorful silken Chinese acrobats returned to Katie's head. Posters in the school's hallways showed flexible bodies making O's, S's, U's and upside down Y's. Other posters presented feet clad in intense green, yellow and red silk slippers leaping high into the air, as if they could fly. Katie feared that she had looked at these posters too long, for images felt free to dance before her eyes whenever they chose to do so.

Why couldn't she line up with the others today, just this once, until she found a new safe harbor? She knew the rules by heart. "Plain people are not allowed to attend assemblies. You must remain behind in the classroom."

It was difficult to follow so many rules: You are not allowed to attend assemblies. You are not allowed to salute the flag. You must not quarrel with others, even if they pick on you.

And wear plain clothing! Katie found this rule particularly painful. She was well aware of her classmates wearing gray flannel pleated skirts topped by soft pink sweaters and strands of pearls, all this with snow white socks tucked into black patent leather shoes.

She felt different only when she went to school, though. At home it was cozy, joyful, where she spent many happy days playing with her brothers and sisters. The pastures were favorite spots, but before venturing into them, they looked to see if the huge bull was back.

He appeared at certain times of the year, and if anyone knew why this was so, they certainly hadn't shared the information with her.

A huge bull was an animal to be feared, for he was a master at pretending to mind his business while grazing in the pasture, oblivious to what went on around him. But no one should be fooled. He knew the exact position of every blade of grass.

The children learned to be careful. They crawled over the gate and sneaked under the fence, keeping a watchful eye on the bull as he ate his grass. They advanced. He ate more grass. Then, one step too close, and they had entered his guarded area.

He let out an ear-piercing bellow. His front hoofs bared a patch of soil as his back hoofs sent it flying. These preliminary moves seemed necessary to load his "cannon," for no sooner were they done when he shot across the pasture straight at them.

"Run! Run!" they screamed to each other. "Run fast." They scampered under the fence or over the gate as the ground trembled under the bull's huge hoofs. Snorts sent hot air down their backs, which they felt just as they leaped to safety.

They found it strange that no matter how far away they were when the bull first noticed them, his charge across the pasture happened so quickly that they always ended up just a leg short of being devoured.

# FLIGHTS OF THE HERONS

But when the bull was elsewhere, this pasture belonged to them.

In happy, carefree summer days, the pasture rang with children's giggles as they played among the colorful blooms of buttercups, Queen Anne's lace, and wild geraniums. Profusely leafed trees of elms and maples placed their branches at just the right height for children to climb, their massive boughs arched in wide, inviting smiles. Chubby, cheerful creeks caressed the children's play-fatigued bare feet as they splashed and cooled in crystal pure water.

In the winter months it was just as much fun, as the hills of the pasture now bloomed with snow and became a sledding paradise. Hills bereft of trees and bushes filled with rows and rows of perfect snow angels in sizes from toddler to teen. Patches of snow gave teeth to the smiling tree boughs as they watched the happy children play. Echoes passed the merriment from hill to hill as if to invite the world to join the joyous sounds of children at play.

As they tired from sledding and making angels, the gurgling sounds of the partially frozen little creek invited the cheeky children to press their faces upon its icy layer. "Come see the awesome pictures I can draw," it seemed to say. The children marveled at the artistry of water deciding whether to freeze or thaw.

Katie helped Rebecca wash and dry the breakfast dishes. Then she dressed for school. As she took an available seat on the bus, her dilemma again preoccupied her. It had all happened on a day much like this, a day when she carried Mama's excuse note in her pocket.

"It's time to line up for the assembly," her teacher said.

Katie asked for permission to go to the bathroom. She happily skipped down the hall and into the bathroom while humming a song.

As she entered the bathroom, she saw Valerie, who was a

few years older than she, at the sink washing her hands. No one else was there.

Katie knew Valerie since they rode the same school bus and greeted her with a cheerful "Hello." So spirited was the greeting that it would have been graciously returned by even the tiniest corner spider. However, Valerie didn't seem to hear it at all.

Katie questioned this lack of acknowledgment, but quickly excused it. Perhaps Valerie was preoccupied with something. Maybe she had trouble with her lessons. Maybe a teacher had spoken sharply to her.

For now, she needed to use the toilet and headed for the stall. All of a sudden, she heard a sharp snort behind her and, for an instant, a vision of the pasture bull flashed before her eyes.

When she turned around, she saw Valerie's large, black pupils pulsing wildly in her flushed, swollen face. Her hot breaths came fast and stormed Katie's skin. She stepped back, trying to get away from the blasts.

"Pull down your panties!" Valerie ordered, her voice grave and deep. Heat poured from Valerie's skin.

The toilet! she thought to herself. She had to get into the toilet stall and somehow slam the door between Valerie and herself.

But Valerie matched her every step.

"Pull down your panties!" Her biting voice warned that dire consequences would follow if her order was not obeyed. Her huge pupils gave her face a look of urgency.

Katie trembled, but what could she do? She must be the lamb, and let the lion devour her, for her Mennonite upbringing taught her to "turn the other cheek." She must not fight back. Not even if it meant her life! With such training, no other thoughts such as "slap her!" or "sock her in the stomach!" entered her mind.

Meekly, between teeny little sobs, she pulled down her panties.

What happened next, Katie later concluded, must have been the result of an angel sent by God, for just then another schoolmate entered the bathroom. Valerie quickly turned around and left the toilet stall, as if nothing had happened. She returned to the sink and again washed her hands.

Somehow Katie managed to lock the toilet door. Dazed, she sat upon the stool. She heard Valerie leave the bathroom. The angel left also. Others came and went, but she could face no one. Finally, there was complete silence. Only then did she exit the bathroom and return to her classroom.

"Mama! Mama!" she exclaimed as she ran into the house after school that day.

She told Mama about the incident, but discreetly omitted the part about why she had gone to the bathroom in the first place. Mama would not have approved of her escaping an embarrassing situation in that way.

Mama did not act surprised at all. Instead, she said, "Katharina, that type of thing happens to us. We're easy to attack because we're different. People view us as beneath them. That's why I tell you to be very careful about walking alone on these country roads. Never, ever go near a car when a stranger stops. If he wants directions, tell him from afar, but don't get near enough to the car that he can grab you. And now, sadly, you have learned that you must never go to the bathroom alone either."

It was time for the Chinese Acrobats to present their astounding and highly entertaining achievements. Mama had written the excuse as usual, but Katie chose not to use it that day. She could no longer go to the bathroom to escape her embarrassment of being different. She didn't want to remain alone in the classroom. And she couldn't think of anything else to do. So she lined up with her classmates.

The performance of the acrobats totally mesmerized

Katie, and, no matter how hard she tried, she could not feel that she had sinned.

***

Katie turned on her IBM computer and started to write.

> *Dear Frank,*
> 
> *How enchantingly you tell the story of your excursion back into your (our!) genealogical history! You made me feel like I was there with you and your mother. Thanks for sharing your wonderful trip with me.*
> 
> *I am extremely grateful to you and your mother for all the hard work you have done in uncovering information about our ancestors. I'm afraid none of my family would ever have known about Johann Gotthard and Pleidelsheim without your efforts.*
> 
> *Your letter had me walking the streets of Pleidelsheim myself. Your quest is contagious, because now I yearn to visit that little town someday too!*
> 
> *Just think! You were in the house in Germany where Johann Gotthard grew up. And now I have a surprise for you. I actually LIVED in Johann's farmhouse in America! When you asked me where I had lived in Columbiana, I thought about it and remembered that the house had been owned by my great-great-grandfather John, whom you know as Johann Gotthard. This is so exciting!*

Katie continued by sharing with Frank most of the story about the assembly and Chinese acrobats, discreetly leaving out the bathroom incident, which seemed a little too intimate to disclose in an e-mail.

She then asked Frank about Hans Reyher.

*I had never heard anything about the Switzerland connection and Hans Reyher. Could you please write and fill me in on this? And just what does it mean when you say he came to Pleidelsheim to claim a "homestead?"*

*Thank you for telling me about your father. I'm sorry he had to die that way. The best medicine for guilt is to share it with others. I hope you'll feel better now that you have told it to me.*

*Also, thanks for the descendants' chart. I have made copies and sent them to my mother, brothers and sisters. It amazes me to see how many of them have been named after our ancestors. And, yes, you are correct in that I was named after my great-great-grandmother. However, everyone calls me Katie except my mother. For some reason, she always uses my full given name.*

*I never go back to Columbiana anymore. It's not that I wouldn't like to, but my family visits seem limited to Pittsburgh. I make sure I return to Pittsburgh every summer to see them.*

*Your thoughts regarding fate and chance intrigue me. I would be interested in your conclusion. Did our paths cross because of fate or chance?*

*Indeed, I do think we have drama in our genealogical roots. It would make a most fascinating book. I'll try to think of an interesting context in which we could present this drama. And, Frank, with your knowledge of German and the Pleidelsheim area, you would be the perfect one to collaborate with on this type of book!*

*I enjoy your letters so very much. Please let me hear again from you soon.*
*With warm regards,*
*Katie.*

She carefully saved the letter, but only to a diskette, which she then took over to Carol's for e-mailing.

# 5.

## HANS REYHER

Frank devoured Katie's e-mail. So she had been born in the same farmhouse that Johann had bought so many years ago! Frank resolved to see it someday, although he assumed it was no longer in the family's possession. He would ask Katie if she knew who bought it. And get directions on how to find it.

He marveled at the vivid descriptions of the farm's pastures—the children's playground. Johann would have walked those same pastures; his children would have played there as well.

Beyond Katie's pasture playground stories, Frank sensed, in the shadows, existed a girl who had experienced hardship. How could it have been otherwise, coming as she did from a family of twelve children? Her father had died when she was much too young, and had left her with feelings of guilt about his death. Yet, she had the capacity to empathize with his situation, and to hope he'd find comfort through sharing his feelings of guilt. He was sure Katie did not flip her hair.

Frank loved the Chinese acrobat story, thinking that he had perhaps seen the same assembly—although a few years earlier, given the difference in their ages. Some assemblies seemed to re-tour every few years. Imagine not being allowed to attend assemblies! What kind of religion would ban something so sinless? Some religious rules seemed to have the sole purpose of inhibiting one's growth.

He loaded his genealogy program and looked up Katie's name. He entered a note that "Katie" was her nickname, entered Kenneth Krauss as her spouse, and Kristine Krauss as her daughter, age: about twenty-one.

Since Katie had asked about Hans, Frank switched over into word processing and contemplated a response. He knew where Hans had lived in Switzerland, his decision to leave, and why.

Upon learning of the Reyhers' Switzerland connection, Frank read extensively about the Thirty Years' War. Some of the books had been written in German. He felt he had grasped the aspirations and the type of experiences a young man such as Hans would have had during that time. Like modern young men, Hans surely had sought independence and the pursuit of happiness.

"Maybe I'll write a fictionalized account," Frank mused. "That would be the perfect vehicle in which to tell Hans Reyher's story."

Soon Frank found himself on a creative roll. He chuckled as the story developed. He couldn't believe it when the clock struck eleven. He decided he'd better get to bed or he'd be worth nothing in the morning. However, by this time he was so stimulated that he was forced to down a stiff whiskey in order to get to sleep.

The next day was especially busy at work. Any other day, he would have stayed after hours to do paperwork. However, the images and objects that had popped into his mind throughout the day now demanded to be put on paper.

He booted up his computer, then opened the file. Hans' story appeared on the screen. After working several hours, he finished, then edited and saved it for attachment.

He composed the following cover letter:

# ESTHER ROYER AYERS

*Dear Cousin Katie,*

*I find it amazing that you were born in the same farmhouse that Johann bought so many years ago. What a shame it is no longer in the family! On one of my free days, I intend to drive to the area and locate the farm. Please give me directions. And do you know who owns this farm today? I would be interested in obtaining permission to see the place, the farmhouse, the barn, the pastures (when the bull's away, naturally) and the gardens.*

*I was captivated by the beauty of the farmland as you've painted it. Now I feel compelled to experience that part of Johann's life for myself, just as my mother and I did for an earlier part of his life on our recent Pleidelsheim trip.*

*I'm afraid I don't know much about farms, as I was raised in the town of Boardman which lies just south of Youngstown. My mother still lives there. It now seems small, compared with Youngstown (itself hardly a metropolis!), to which I moved after completing my education.*

*Your description of the Chinese acrobats reminded me of an assembly I had attended at school in my youth. I, too, was mesmerized by their performance, but had forgotten all about it. Your portrayal reawakened long-lost memories and caused me to feel the same excitement I had felt as a child.*

*Somehow that brings me back to the timeless—and timely—question of fate versus chance. Whether it was through fate or chance, someone dealt us some cards. Cousin Katie, not only were we dealt these cards, but so were our ancestors. And how our ancestors played their cards fascinates me.*

*For instance, Johann Gotthard's escape from the Kingdom of Wuerttemberg in 1819 was prompted by a fateful situation. His cards said, "Either be a mercenary for the king for a few years, or leave your loved ones and* secure environment for the unknowns and the dangers of a distant land." Imagine making a decision like that!

In America during the height of the Viet Nam war, many a heart was wrenched by the fate of draft-age boys who fled to Canada lest they end up in a war they didn't approve of. But these boys, unlike Johann Gotthard, had no problem getting to their destination, no real problem with settling in (the Canadians were accommodating), and no problem communicating—instantaneously, by telephone—with the loved ones they left behind. And the war they were escaping was at least one in which their own country was a belligerent!

In fact, fate dealt cards much earlier in our ancestors' lives. Remember when I wrote about learning in Pleidelsheim of Hans Reyher? He was the first of our Reyher ancestors in Germany, having emigrated to what was then called the "German lands" from Switzerland in 1654.

Pleidelsheim had lost ninety percent of its population in the just-concluded Thirty Years' War. As the small Protestant town tried to attract new inhabitants, Hans was enticed by a recruiting advertisement. We can only fantasize the details, of course, but Hans himself must have been confronted with a fateful decision.

I've spent the past several evenings thinking about how a fictionalized story of Hans' might play out. It's in my head, and I can't resist sharing it with you. I hope you will forgive me for becoming an "arm chair" storyteller. Maybe I have too many evening hours that would otherwise be depressingly empty.

My story, "Flight of the Heron," is attached. Sorry that it got so long. I was just trying to demonstrate what I have in mind, and got carried away. I am sure you will see umpteen ways of spicing up the narrative. That's why I am hopeful you will agree to collaborate with me. Let me know what you think. By the way, do you remember my telling *you in the first letter that "Reyher" is the German word for "Heron?" That's the reason for the title.*

*You said in your last letter that you never go back to Columbiana but that you do visit your mother, brothers and sisters in Pittsburgh every summer. I could meet you there, as it's an easy drive from Youngstown to Pittsburgh.*

*I have a fair amount of control over my schedule and am reasonably confident that anytime you suggest will be fine. You can't imagine how eager I am to meet you and discuss this project in depth.*
*With warm regards,*
*Frank*

\*\*\*

ATTACHMENT

### *Flight of the Heron*

"Stop staring into space and get to work." The loud voice rudely ended Hans Jr.'s daydream.

"Yes, father," he sighed, picking up the hoe to resume his weeding of the potato field. Why couldn't he have been the first-born son? His older brother Peter had it made. He stood not only to inherit the family farm, but also to get advanced schooling.

"These days a young man needs to run fast just to keep up," his father, Hans Reyher Sr., liked to say. Translated, this meant: Without a good education, Peter might squander his inheritance even with the best of intentions.

Hans Jr. thrust the hoe savagely into the weed-infested soil as he thought, "I'm at least as smart as Peter. It's not fair how he's favored." Yet Hans Jr. knew his father was not being arbitrary.

Primogeniture was now the law in Switzerland, or at least

in the part in which the Reyhers resided. Employing the "direct democracy" for which the country later was to become greatly admired, the "burghers" (those who could vote)—themselves mostly property-owners as a result of being firstborn sons—had decided that the ever-smaller farms resulting from a divided inheritance created double trouble. They could not be managed profitably, and the process of dividing the property, with subsequent perils of propinquity, typically led to disputes among siblings.

These disputes were disturbing, and in some cases even undermining, the internal peace the Swiss had come to regard as their greatest asset. And peace, Hans Jr. knew, was indeed an asset. He shuddered at the thought of the atrocities other German-speaking peoples had suffered in the Great War, as the Thirty Years' War (fought from 1618 to 1648) was then known. News reached their little village, Ruswil, only indirectly, and so perhaps was suspect. But in the nearby urban center of Lucerne one could get up-to-date, reliable reports.

Only a few years before, when Hans Jr. for the first time had joined his father in the pubs there, he personally heard travelers report on the horrible scenes they had witnessed in the Rhine valley and elsewhere. "Whole towns were razed," they said. "The only survivors were those lucky enough to have been absent when the attack occurred."

Almost no one, least of all in neutral Switzerland, could exactly recall the issues that led to the war. Religion—specifically, the struggle for power and influence between the still relatively new Lutherans, Calvinists and the established Roman church—was only one. There were others of equal or greater importance.

If the causes of the Great War were ambiguous, the results were not. The princes and bishops, who made the decisions and commanded the armies, had been largely spared the agonies of the war. True, they perhaps lost a district or two, or were forced to cut back on their winter vacations in

Tuscany for awhile, but their lives had gone on pretty much as before.

It was the common people—very much like the Reyhers in Ruswil—who had perished and/or lost everything they owned. The killing and depredations seemingly went on forever. A whole generation grew up knowing nothing but war.

So Hans Jr. had no difficulty understanding that peace warranted sacrifices. If primogeniture helped keep the peace, far be it from him to object. Occasionally, land became available—at a stiff price—when the owner left no heir. But, even if he had the money (which he did not), another barrier would have kept Hans Jr. from buying: Ruswil was a predominantly Catholic area of Switzerland. As Protestants, the Reyhers were happy just to be tolerated; they certainly were not going to risk their very lives in an effort to expand their land holdings.

Still, Hans Jr. wished there was some way to turn his sacrifice into a blessing. He recalled his mother saying whenever something negative happened to him, "Who knows what good might come of it?" (That, Katie, is a direct translation from German. In America, we might say, "Every cloud has a silver lining.") How could he possibly profit from his present situation? He asked himself that question dozens of times, but never found the answer.

Hans Jr. looked around excitedly as he tied his horse to a railing. It was his first solo in Lucerne. Peter was away on his annual military training. Hans Sr., bedridden with the flu, had asked his younger son to do the regular run to market surplus items from the farm: eggs, strawberries, and asparagus at this time of the year.

In a pinch, the Reyhers could always unload surpluses in Ruswil, but at a substantially lower price. Such costly compromises were no longer necessary now that Hans Jr. was almost twenty and had previous experience on selling trips with his father. Women, of course, were deemed to be ill-suited for such tasks.

Hans Jr. went about his business methodically. From the earlier visits he knew all the buyers in town. And, unlike his father, he was prepared to spend a lot of time haggling. As a result, he got better prices for the produce than his father had been expecting. "That'll show him who has the brains in the family," Hans Jr. muttered to himself.

Having enriched the family, he decided to take his personal commission. In another first solo for him, he headed for the "Alpenstubl," his favorite of the pubs he had frequented with his father.

"Beer, please," Hans Jr. said, trying to look nonchalant. He noticed a man, obviously a traveler, sitting there with some papers.

"Hey, there, young man, please join me," the traveler said, gesturing to the empty chair next to him.

His parents' warnings about strangers flashed through his mind. Hans Jr. at first hesitated, but then thought to himself, "I'm grown up now, and what can happen in this pub?" So he said, "Thank you, sir, I'd be happy to," took his beer, and sat next to the man.

"Where are you from?" the man asked.

"A little village a few miles away called Ruswil," Hans Jr. replied.

"Are you a farmer?"

"My father is, and I help out, of course."

"But you don't think of yourself as a farmer?"

"To be a farmer," Hans Jr. replied, "you have to have a farm. I will never have a farm."

"So you're not the oldest son," the man said. Obviously he knew about primogeniture in Switzerland.

"No," Hans Jr. replied, disconsolately.

"Well, then, maybe you'd be interested in this." The man pointed to the circulars next to him. "Can you read?"

"Of course," Hans Jr. replied, showing a flash of anger as he took the circular. "Almost everyone in this part of Switzerland can read and write."

In reality, Hans Jr. had little experience with reading anything other than simple ledgers needed for their farm business and the treasured family-heirloom Bible from one of the original two-hundred-year-old Gutenberg presses. Nonetheless, the circular had big print and mostly easy words. He read:

### *HOMESTEADERS WANTED!*

The town of Pleidelsheim, in the Duchy of Wuerttemberg, is seeking men under 30 of the Lutheran or Calvinist persuasion, with or without accompanying families, as settlers to replace population lost during the Great War.

Each qualifying settler will be assigned 20 morgens [a morgen = ca. an acre] of land and suitable temporary living quarters. If the settler works the land and remains in Pleidelsheim for at least five years, he will receive clear title allowing him thereafter to dispose of the land as he sees fit.

Pleidelsheim is located on the east bank of the Neckar River about 100 miles upstream from the Rhine, of which the Neckar is a tributary. The nearest city, Stuttgart, capital of the Duchy, lies about eight miles to the south.

Some small plots are available in the ancient vineyards on the hills overlooking the river. However, most of the land for homesteading purposes is on the plain east of the river.

Those interested should write to the Burgermeister (mayor) of Pleidelsheim. The letter should include the applicant's full name, current residence, and church affiliation (including the pastor's name). The letter should be given to the agent circulating this notice. Successful applicants will be notified late this summer, i.e., by September 1, 1653, and will have up to six months thereafter to take possession of their assigned homesteads.

Hans Jr. rubbed his eyes as if in a daze. Had he read correctly? Twenty morgens of land? "What exactly does 'homestead' mean?" he asked, needing time to gather his thoughts.

"That's just a fancy way of saying you get land without having to pay for it," the man replied. "It's like squatters' rights, except that squatters just move in, uninvited. Homesteaders are invited and sometimes even carefully selected, as in this case."

"How do I know this offer is for real?" Hans Jr. asked suspiciously, looking for the catch in what appeared to be an unbelievable opportunity. "And how do I know you are really the agent mentioned in the circular?"

The man pulled a scroll out of his bag and unrolled it. "Take a look," he said.

With difficulty, Hans Jr. read the letter of introduction from the Burgermeister of Pleidelsheim, written in immaculate long-hand. What most struck him was the fancy red wax seal. He had never seen a document that looked more convincingly official.

"What is more," the man said, "why would I make all of this up? The terms of the offer do not stipulate any sort of payment to anyone. If I were dishonest, surely I would be asking for at least a few *gulden* for administrative costs. The fact is, Pleidelsheim is paying me a commission for each qualified person I recruit, but the person must arrive there first. And if he submits a complaint about me that turns out to be justified, the town will pay me nothing."

Hans Jr. nodded, finding the explanation eminently reasonable. Still, the questions kept coming. "Is it dangerous in Pleidelsheim?" he asked.

"No longer," the man replied. "Pleidelsheim *per se* was never really a dangerous place, although the area has its highwaymen like everywhere else. The suffering—wanton killing and destruction—came when conflicting armies passed through during the war. With the coming of the Westphalian peace, the armies went home. Of course, it takes time to reestablish order and basic services, but that's pretty well accomplished by now. After all, it's been five years since the treaties were signed."

"Do you really think I'd have a chance?" Hans Jr. asked, now increasingly enthused. "There must be thousands of young men like me that you've approached."

"Good point," the man said, "but remember what the war did throughout the German lands. The fact is, there are many 'Pleidelsheims.' Practically all of them are seeking settlers for the same reason Pleidelsheim is, and are also encountering the same skepticism. People are suspicious. They know it's not normal to be offered something for nothing. Besides, no one can really believe the war is over.

"But take it from me, young man. Skepticism or not, the first homesteaders are beginning to pour into the German lands, and, as they write back to their families and report positive things, or at least refute some of the negatives, the word will spread and this movement will snowball. You have your chance now. In fact, I'd call it a God-given opportunity. Next year may well be too late."

One of his father's little sayings came into Hans Jr.'s mind: "A good salesman will convince you his bulls give milk." There has to be downside, he thought. Still, from what he had heard about the war and its effects, the man's arguments made sense.

Hans Jr. took a deep breath. He remembered that "good" his mother had tried to convince him might be hidden behind the bad things happening to him. Maybe he had at last stumbled onto it.

"Thank you, sir," he said, taking the circular and getting up to leave. "I will give it very serious consideration. How can I reach you, if I decide to apply?"

"I'll be back through in another week," he said. "Just stop in at the Alpenstubl again."

Never in anyone's memory had the Reyher household seen tension as occurred in the following few days. Hans Jr. returned from his marketing trip, knowing instinctively that his cause would be best served by direct talk and arguments. Beating around the bush just ruined the bush, he mused. So, immediately after basking in his father's praise for the unexpected windfall profit from sale of the produce, Hans Jr. dropped his bombshell.

At first Hans Sr. could not believe his son was serious. Then he refused to discuss the subject. But in the end the rules of family democracy prevailed.

Hans Jr. pressed his case relentlessly, and his mother, having become convinced herself, told her husband to stop being so stubborn. The clincher came when Peter returned from his training and promptly supported his brother. But discussion was one thing; approval was another. If Hans Sr. was opposed, everyone knew Hans Jr.'s chances of successfully pulling off his venture were greatly reduced.

Every evening for the next four days the discussion went the same way. Hans Jr. patiently repeated his conversation with the agent. Hans Sr. reviewed the Pleidelsheim circular again, and said, "I still don't understand it. In this world you don't get something for nothing."

Finally Hans Sr. said, "There's no sense talking about it any more. I'll think about it and let you know in the morning."

Lying in bed that night, Hans Sr. went over everything in his mind. His respect for Hans Jr.'s judgment had grown steadily as his son matured. And Hans Jr. had never before been so adamant about anything.

At his wife's instigation, Hans Sr. struggled to look at the issue from Hans Jr.'s perspective. He gradually came to accept the argument that his son really did have little to lose and potentially a lot to gain in applying for a homestead in Pleidelsheim.

Assuming he evaded the highwaymen (which, Hans Sr. ruefully admitted, wasn't always possible even in orderly Switzerland), the worst outcome for Hans Jr. would be to arrive and find the Pleidelsheim authorities unwilling to honor their offer. Then he would have to sell his supplies, possibly at a loss, and return empty-handed. He would certainly be out-of-pocket for the costs of the travel. But if the offer was honored—and this possibility certainly existed—Hans Jr. would have a farm almost as big as theirs in Ruswil. Over time, he might even be able to buy more land.

Hans Sr. sighed. The process of family democracy again led to a rational decision, but now he traded a load on his mind for a lump in his throat. In the morning he would wish Hans Jr. Godspeed—knowing full well that his departure meant the family would rarely, if ever, see him again.

Hans Jr.'s application was accepted, and by early February he was ready to start his journey, which, the agent told him would take about six weeks. He wanted to arrive in Pleidelsheim early enough to have a chance of reaping a full season of crops.

He was, he thought, as well prepared as anyone could be. With the money he had saved, and part of a five-hundred gulden loan from his father, he bought the latest farm implements, seeds, and almanacks. He packed everything in sturdy new trunks. He even took a property insurance policy from one of those fast-talking agents from Zurich, just in case the feared highwaymen showed up unexpectedly somewhere along the way.

After tearful farewells to his family, who came to Lucerne to see him off, Hans Jr. (who, once out of his father's shadow, dropped the "Jr.") boarded the boat that would take him down the Reuss and Aare rivers as far as Waldshut, on the Rhine. They set off, and the initial portion of the trip on swollen rivers proved to be both treacherous and tiring. Hans admired the boatsmen, who regularly subjected themselves to great danger for the sake of their passengers.

River travel was also hard work. Repeatedly, at boulder-filled rapids (where dams and hydroelectric power stations can be found today), they were forced to portage: to unload the boat and laboriously carry cargo and the boat down river. On clear days, the assignment was tough enough. If it rained—or worse, snowed—life became miserable for everybody, including the handful of passengers.

After a week they reached the mighty Rhine. There Hans transferred to a larger boat for the passage into the German lands. Although there were also several treacherous rapids between Waldshut and Basle, the water was deep enough so that, albeit with a bit of excitement, boats could pass without portaging. Thereafter, the travel became less eventful and moved much more quickly.

Within another week they arrived at the mouth of the Neckar at Mannheim. Mileage-wise, ninety percent of the trip was over. From that point on, however, the travel would be upstream, against the current, a current that was just as swollen as it had been in Switzerland. Half of the entire trip time lay ahead.

Hans might have disembarked at Karlsruhe and taken the land route to Pleidelsheim, but this was not Rome. There were no paved roads and it was spring. Who knew how often a heavily-laden carriage would have gotten stuck in the mud? The land route would have been a perfect setting for high-waymen to do Hans in. No, he had no stomach for such adventures. The river route might take longer, theoretically, but it also was much safer.

Again a change of boats. A total of six oarsmen were now on board for the Neckar. The boat had a sail, but it was used mainly to speed up the trip downstream. Going upstream, it was of little use. Not only were the winds irregular, but the Neckar was too narrow in most areas to permit tacking.

For much of the distance to Pleidelsheim the boat could be pulled by mules. But wherever the river bank was too steep for a tow path, the oarsmen had to row, and row hard. The trick was to hug the shore where the downstream current was considerably slower. Of course, that procedure increased the possibility of crashing into boulders along the shore or of going aground at some points. Lest the oarsmen tire of their toil, they could look forward, for a change of pace, to portaging at a few points.

Farming might be a risky occupation, with a panoply of potential natural disasters, but Hans knew now that he would never trade it for the oarsmen's job. Nor would he ever again complain about the cost of river travel.

Finally, six weeks and two days after his departure from Lucerne, Hans arrived safely in Pleidelsheim. Several men and a couple of young boys appeared at the docking point to meet the boat. They helped Hans with his trunks and took him immediately to the burgermeister, as custom dictated in relatively small towns.

Hans found the town a great deal more run-down than he had expected. He noticed that many homes were burnt-out hulks, while a few others appeared completely uninhabited.

The group took Hans to the Rathaus (municipal building), where the burgermeister soon received him. Hans showed him his acceptance letter. The burgermeister looked it over quickly, extended his hand, and then said, "Welcome and congratulations, Herr Reyher." It was March 21—the vernal equinox—in 1654, when Hans's life in Pleidelsheim began.

True to his abilities and habits, Hans worked hard and, despite some early bad luck, began to prosper. And true to its commitment, the city gave him his land title in a special ceremony on March 21, 1659. It simultaneously made him, at the age of just twenty-five, a burgher with full voting rights. Hans was popular, and everyone agreed that the recruitment program had been well worth the cost in his case.

In the next couple of years, Hans continued to work hard and managed to buy one of the nicer homes in Pleidelsheim. His gamble in leaving Ruswil had paid off as handsomely as anyone could have imagined. Now it was time for him to return, to see his family, and to take steps to fill a major void in his life. He needed a wife.

After the harvest in 1661, Hans left his farm in the care of a trusted assistant and started on a five-month journey. He returned in mid-March 1662 with the future Frau Reyher, Anna Steiner, the daughter of Joseph. As the Steiners were Catholic (no marriageable Protestant girls had been available), Hans and Anna had no choice but to be married in Pleidelsheim. The wedding took place on April 29, 1662. Within a year, on April 17, 1663, their daughter, Anna Barbara, was born. As fate would have it, Anna died in infancy, but, on March 31, 1665, the Reyhers had a baby boy, Johann Caspar (who also came to be known as "Hans").

Hans Reyher had no further children, unlike many Reyhers in later generations who had very large families. But his son lived to become a baker, opened an inn called the "Stern" and in 1710, after his first wife had died, married Christine Magdalene Uschalk, the daughter of the Ochsen proprietor [do you remember these names from my Pleidelsheim story, Katie?] Although the girl was thirty years younger than Johann Caspar, she bore him at least four sons and two daughters. Thus Hans Reyher from Ruswil ended up starting a dynasty.

***

Frank attached the Hans Reyher story file to his cover letter, then e-mailed the entire message to Katie. He wondered whether she would have any problem downloading the attachment.

It was now well after 11 p.m., and Frank decided he'd better get some sleep. To relax, he turned on the stereo and listened to a bit of Mozart while sipping another nightcap. "This has got to stop," he said to himself. He rarely had a drink two nights in a row. But then again, it had been years since he had so much fun.

# 6

## KITTEN

The phone rang. "Katie," said Carol, "you have an e-mail and this time it has an attachment."

"Oh, can I come over right away and get it?"

"Sure, but I must warn you. If that guy is going to write you a book again, you'd better bring along some paper. I only have about a dozen sheets left before I have to go to the store and get some more."

"His name is Frank, Carol, not 'that guy.'"

"Oh, getting touchy, huh? Wonderful! Maybe we're finally making some progress. See you shortly."

Katie remembered how long Frank's report on the Pleidelsheim trip had been, but doubted this would be a repeat performance. Nevertheless, she picked up a package of computer paper on her way to Carol's.

She printed Frank's cover letter. It alone was extensive. But the attachment! She was glad she brought additional paper along. When the printer finished, she made a neat pile, then took it home to read.

After she read the cover letter, she mentally responded to his desire to visit the farm and the pastures.

She'd grasp his warm hand and run through the meadows with him. She'd lie with him among the sweet field flowers and inhale the intoxicating aromas. She'd wrap her arms around him, and together they'd float to the heavens. They'd soar from cloud to cloud and play peek-a-boo behind the white fluffiness. Would he ever catch her?

Probably the first time he tried, she smiled.

Then she read the attachment. She laughed at Frank's playfulness in the Hans Reyher story. So, he's trying his hand at fiction, she grinned. Then frowned. He's done a good job at it too! Actually, too good! It caused an uneasiness to lap at her fingers, her toes, her heart edges. She would have to tell him he really didn't need her collaboration in writing a book.

But she couldn't do that. Not when she needed him so much. To soften the coarseness in her life. To put the sparkle back into her eyes. To provide her with the strength she needed to make it through one single day.

"I'm sorry, Frank," she said to herself, "but for the first time in my life, I'm going to be dishonest." Since it was a sin of omission, rather than commission, she hoped God would forgive her.

The kitchen clock struck four. It was time to start dinner.

Because of the sheer volume, Katie no longer hid Frank's letters between the kitchen plates. She had found a better spot, a place closer to her heart. She took the story of Hans Reyher and carefully hid it under the perfumed paperliner in her lingerie drawer. There it joined Frank's other correspondence, which by now, created quite a bulge in an intimate compartment.

She returned to the kitchen to start dinner, then noticed the yellow Post-it stuck on the refrigerator door. She had forgotten about it, but knew what it said. "Kitten. I have a meeting after work and won't be home until six. Love, Ken."

Kitten! How she hated that name! She returned mentally to the day she first met Ken. It was the year after she graduated from high school.

# FLIGHTS OF THE HERONS

***

After getting her high school degree, Katie had enrolled at the University of Pittsburgh. While her academic scholarship covered basic costs, she worked as a waitress for money to pay for personal expenses. Her most recent employer was Klein's Seafood Restaurant on Fourth Avenue in downtown Pittsburgh, known for its great seafood. She worked the noontime hours when businessmen and lawyers from nearby offices came in for lunch. The pay was lousy, but the superb tips made it worthwhile.

On a warm April day three well-dressed men in dark suits, white shirts and dark, narrow ties entered the restaurant. Since Katie was busy waiting on tables, she gave the trio no more than a fleeting glance.

The head-waitress escorted and sat the three men at an empty table in Katie's section. Katie was unaware that one of these men stared continuously at her legs as he was seated.

As she approached their table, this same man now stared at her name tag. She was accustomed to customers looking at her badge, but had never had one *stare* at it. It made her uncomfortable, nevertheless, she kindly asked, "Would you like a drink before lunch?"

"Katie Reyher," the man read her badge. "I don't like the name Katie. I think I'll call you Kitten. I haven't seen you here before. How long have you worked here?"

"I started two weeks ago, sir," she said.

"Oh, don't call me 'sir.' Call me Ken. Okay Kitten?"

Katie lowered her eyes. "I'm really not supposed to call our guests by their first names. I'm to use 'sir' or 'Mr.' That's what I've been told."

"Oh, forget that. It's all right for you to call me Ken. And this is Don and Jack. They don't mind if you call them by their first names either. Do you guys?"

"We don't mind. Please do."

"Well, I'm not supposed to, but if you insist, I'm sure my boss won't mind." Her voice was as soft as a butterfly wing in flight.

"Now to answer your question, Kitten. Yes, we'd each like a martini. Extra dry. Two olives in each. We like olives. Bring the martinis. Then we'll order lunch."

As Katie left the table she became aware that the men were looking at her legs. She heard Ken say, "Purr, purr, purrrr-fect!" The three men rolled with laugher.

A few minutes later when she returned with their drinks, she saw their eyes again riveted on her legs. Troubled, she wondered, "What's wrong with my legs?" Her discomfort caused her to spill a little of Ken's martini when she set the glass in front of him.

"Kitten, are we making you nervous?" he chuckled.

"A little, I guess."

"You saw us looking at your legs, didn't you?"

"Y—Yes."

"And you're wondering what's wrong with your legs, aren't you?" Ken looked at the other two, and they burst into laughter.

Katie blushed. She wished she could have melted into the floor.

"Oh, now we've upset the kitten. Boys, enough teasing of this beautiful young lady. Let's tell her why we're looking at her legs.

"We work for the Keystone Advertising Agency. A week ago we received a huge contract from DuPont to do an advertisement for seamless nylon hosiery. We talked this very morning about where we would find a model with perfect legs. Then, we come in here for lunch and find the legs we're looking for. Kitten, you have the perfect legs for advertising hosiery."

"I-I do?" Katie blushed more. Then to get her mind off

all this, she asked them if they had chosen what they wanted for lunch.

Ken ordered for them: "We'll have the special, and another martini all around."

"Be right back," she said. Katie placed the martini order with the bartender, then walked to the kitchen with the meal order.

Jenny, the only other waitress on duty during lunchtime noticed how flushed and breathless she was. "What's wrong with you?" she asked.

"Nothing really. You know how some of these businessmen like to flirt. Boy, I've got a table that is really laying it on. I'll just try to be aloof."

She returned shortly with their martinis. As she approached their table, she heard them say practically in unison, "Yep! We've got the right one."

A few minutes later she returned with their meal. For some reason, now they said nothing to her. "Good," she thought. "Maybe they've finally forgotten about my legs."

She filled their water glasses and asked them if they wanted another martini. "No, thanks." they said. They didn't look at her legs. In fact, they behaved like perfect gentlemen as they ate their lunch.

It left her edgy. "First they unduly compliment me on my legs, now they ignore me. What am I to think?"

She cleared away their plates and asked if they would like some dessert and coffee. "No dessert," they said, "but coffee would be fine."

She returned with cups for all of them. After pouring the coffee, she asked if they would like anything else. "No, just the bill," they said.

Then Ken spoke. "Kitten, we've been talking. How would you like to make some money with those long, slim legs of yours? Could you come over and see me tomorrow at, say, 10:00 in the morning?"

"I-I have classes in the morning and then start work here at eleven. I only work lunch hours, though, so I'm finished at two, or two-thirty usually. I could be in your office at three."

"If it suits you at three, then I'll clear off anything else that might be on my calendar. So it's set then. You'll be there at three. Here's my card. It'll give you the address, which is just a block down the street. You won't have any trouble finding it."

"I'll be there," said Katie.

They paid their bill and left a ten-dollar tip, more than she had ever received before.

"Oh, I'm so stupid," she later told herself. "I didn't even find out what I should wear. Should I wear a suit, like one wears to an office? Or maybe a dress, as a model would wear?"

She asked Jenny later when she reported what had transpired over the lunch hour. "For crying out loud, Katie," said Jenny, "he's only interested in your legs. Wear whatever shows your legs off best."

"What about stockings? Should I wear stockings since I'll be getting dressed up for this ad?"

"I wouldn't. You'll just have to take them off when you get there, then put on the seamless for the ad. It might be awkward."

It was hard for Katie to keep her mind on her lectures the next morning and even harder for her to serve the lunchtime crowd. She finished at two-thirty, then changed into a dress she thought would best show her legs. She brushed her hair and freshened her makeup. At precisely three o'clock she walked into the front door of Suite 32, Keystone Advertising Agency.

A receptionist greeted her warmly, "You must be Katie Reyher."

"Yes, I am."

"Mr. Krauss told me you'd be coming at three. Come with me, please."

The receptionist led her down a hall lined with six glass

doors, each of them displaying a man's name painted in gold. Finally, Katie saw one that read, "Kenneth Krauss, Vice President." She gasped.

The receptionist opened the door. "Mr. Krauss, Miss Reyher."

Ken arose from behind his desk, extended a hand, and invited her to take a chair across the room. She sat down, gently crossing her legs at the ankle. She noticed Ken watched her every move.

"I didn't know you were a Vice President. Your card...."

"Oh, that card. I'm having new ones made up," said Ken.

"I've made arrangements with our best photographer to be here this afternoon," he continued. "You won't really have to do anything. Naturally, we'll pay you."

Katie knew she should ask how much she'd be paid, but it made her feel unsophisticated to do so. What did she know about business operations anyway? The pay, undoubtedly, was set at so-and-so much per hour times however long it took. She was sure it would be fair.

"Come right this way, Kitten." Katie followed him through an office back door into a room filled with huge cameras. She heard an exchange of words between Ken and the photographer, but couldn't make out what they said. Then Ken invited her to come with him over to where a large black cloth covered what appeared to be a chair.

"Should I sit here?" asked Katie.

Ken burst out laughing. "Oh, no, Kitten," he said. "I don't want you to *sit*. We want to see the back of your legs. This is an ad for seamless hosiery. Lean across the back of the chair."

"But I don't have any stockings on. Shouldn't I be wearing seamless hosiery for the ad?"

Ken laughed again. "I love your innocence, Kitten. We'll put makeup on your legs to simulate hosiery."

Katie leaned across the chair with the back of her legs

facing the photographer. Ken walked across the room and looked. "Pretty good, Kitten. I'll be right back."

A few seconds later, Ken returned with the receptionist. "She'll put the leg makeup on you," he said.

The photographer summoned Ken. Again Katie could not hear their conversation. However, Ken looked at her feet, then left the room.

When he returned, he carried a pair of black suede pumps with the highest heels she had ever seen. "Put these on her," he said to the receptionist.

Katie had difficulty walking in the pumps. Fortunately, she had only a few steps to turn around, then lean over the back of the chair. Ken asked the photographer. "Everything okay now?"

"Her legs are too close together. They should be spaced at least six inches apart."

Katie heard that and did so.

"Her skirt needs to be inched up a little."

Katie pulled her skirt up just a little. The receptionist pulled it up higher.

"Perfect! Now hold it there." Katie saw the flash of the camera and heard the change of plates so many times, she lost count.

The photographer finally announced, "Superb! Superb!" Katie took that to mean it must have gone well, and with such a stack of plates, well, she couldn't possibly have known what he wanted with all those.

"Tell you what, Kitten," said Ken, "let me take you to dinner tonight to show you how much I appreciate your hard work."

Ken was a thin man of average height. His dark brown eyes matched the color of his hair. His full lips rested on his square jaw. Katie never noticed Ken's personal features, however. She saw his business suit and tie, his gold-lettered name on his office door followed by the words, "Vice President." All this left her wishing for a fan.

"Did you drive?" Ken asked.

"Drive? Oh, yes." Her brain struggled to reconnect.

"Tell you what we'll do then. I'll get a cab to take us to the restaurant and then return us here. That way you won't have to worry about getting into a car with a stranger, which I don't consider myself to be, but you should. I know girls worry about that, and rightfully so. There are a lot of men out there you shouldn't trust."

His words reassured Katie and made her feel protected.

On their way to the restaurant, Ken told her that he was thirty-four and had never been married or even had a serious romance. "Just couldn't find the right girl," he said.

Dinner conversation turned out to be a monologue by Ken. With obvious pride, he told Katie he had been high school valedictorian and graduated from college summa cum laude. Even now, he declared matter-of-factly, he was far more intelligent than the others at the ad agency, including the president. Then, with unrestrained ebullience, he boldly announced that he would *definitely* be a millionaire by the time he was forty. All this fluffing and flashing of brilliantly colored feathers in front of Katie's eyes set off a cascade of electrical and chemical reactions in her head.

For the next six weeks, Katie was caught up in a whirlwind. Ken took her to the finest restaurants, to dances, to plays. She did things she had never done before in her life, and Ken loved her wide-eyed innocence.

Then Ken called one morning and said, "Put on your prettiest dress and smile, because tonight is going to be very special for you and me. I'll pick you up at five."

Katie couldn't contain her excitement. She talked with Jenny between orders. "You're glowing!" said Jenny. "You've really gone over the edge with Ken. Better be careful!"

"Why do you say that?"

"Let's just say this. A person who has ever been mauled by a dog has super-sensitive cells, cells sensitized to the point that they recognize a mean dog before the first snarl or baring of teeth."

"What are you talking about?" asked Katie, but before she could receive an answer, the chef indicated her lunch order was ready for delivery.

At three o'clock Katie finished work for the day. She still couldn't imagine what Ken had planned. They had done so many wonderful things together. What could make this evening so unique? Maybe he was finally going to introduce her to his mother and father, his family. He had promised that she would meet them soon. Katie was still trying to guess what was in store for her when Ken arrived promptly at five.

"I've been trying all day to guess what you've planned," she said.

"And what have you come up with, Kitten?"

"I think I'm going to finally meet your family."

"Wrong," said Ken, somewhat irritated. "I told you you'll get to meet them someday. I don't see why you keep talking about that. It's no big deal. At least not to me."

It was a big deal to Katie, however. She introduced Ken to her family and had felt incomplete until she had done so. To be fair, of course, she must remember that she was from an Old Order family, which was always close. Maybe this wasn't true for families of the world. She had much to learn.

"I give up then, Ken. I was sure that was it."

"What I have planned is much more important than meeting my family."

His response made Katie uncomfortable, for she remembered a favorite saying of her mother's: "The way a man treats his mother is the way he'll treat his wife." Deep inside, she felt it necessary to watch Ken and his mother interact.

But then, maybe that was an Old Order saying. Ken had never given her any reason to be suspicious of him. He had treated her like a perfect gentleman from the beginning. Indeed, he had never asked for anything more than a goodnight kiss. Quite unlike the other boys she had dated.

"I can't think of anything else," Katie finally said.

Ken just laughed. "You'll know before the evening is out."

The car charged up hill after hill. "Where are we going?" asked Katie.

"Someplace you've never been before."

"Oh, I can't imagine where that might be."

"You'll know what *fantastic* means before this evening is out."

As they reached the top, the exclusive LeMont restaurant—with its lofty, envious perch on a choice hill overlooking the city of Pittsburgh—unfolded before Katie's eyes. While drinking in the beauty of the place, a valet opened her door and extended a helpful hand.

The maitre d' appeared to be expecting their arrival. He quickly escorted them to the finest section of the dining room and seated them into a spacious round booth. Huge glass windows overlooked the intersection of three marvelous rivers, the Monongahela, Allegheny and Ohio. Katie remembered from her geography class that this was actually the birthplace of the Ohio.

While she watched the rivers weave by the window, a bottle of champagne was brought to their table. It was the first time she had tasted champagne. The bubbles tickled her nose and made her laugh.

"Wow! What a nice surprise!" Katie exclaimed.

"Oh, this isn't the surprise," said Ken. "The surprise is still to come."

Soon bread and salads appeared at their table. "I haven't seen the menu," said Katie. "How do they know what I want?"

Ken laughed at her innocence.

A cart with a copper skillet was wheeled to their table as the chef began preparations for steak Diane. He poured something from a bottle into the hot pan, which hissed and caused bright orange tongues of fire to lick the air. The flames mesmerized Katie; the aroma put her into a state of bliss.

"Mademoiselle?" asked the waiter, as he placed the steak in front of her. "Bourgognaise?"

"Please," said Katie, although she had no idea of what she had asked for.

The chef poured a little sauce onto the meat, then decorated her plate with red potatoes, orange carrots and green broccoli. He stepped back to admire his masterpiece, then pronounced it, "Mademoiselle!"

"Monsieur?" He then proceeded to make the same mouth-watering masterpiece for Ken.

Throughout the dinner Katie tried to imagine what the surprise might be, and Ken laughed at all her guesses.

After dinner Ken decided to forego his customary cognac. Instead he ordered their finest bottle of Moët & Chandon. A fresh ice bucket was quickly set up at their table. The waiter uncorked the bottle and poured them each a glass. Then Katie heard Ken say, "Time to bring it now."

He returned shortly, his gloved hand balancing a silver tray high above his head. He stopped in front of Katie, then slowly lowered the tray until she saw it held a magazine.

"What's this?"

"This month's *Vogue* magazine," Ken replied.

"Yes, I can see that, but why?" Katie was laughing now, liberated by the champagne.

"Go ahead. Take it. Open it to the page that's marked with a red rose."

Katie did as she was told, then forced herself to blink twice to make sure she wasn't dreaming, or had too much champagne. But there was no denying it. A full-page photograph of her legs unfolded before her eyes. "I—I," was all she could say.

"Actually, this hasn't been published yet," Ken explained.

"It takes time to get these things into magazines, but the ad is done and DuPont has bought it, so an ad exactly like this will appear soon in *Vogue*. What do you think?"

"I'-I'-I'-I'm speechless."

Ken laughed. "That's only part of the surprise. This is the rest." He pulled a small package wrapped in gold paper from his jacket pocket. "Go ahead. Open it."

Katie carefully unwrapped the package. Inside she found a small box with a hinged top. When she opened it, she saw a huge diamond nestled in blue velvet.

"I-I." Its dazzle, or the champagne, or maybe both took her voice.

However, she didn't need to speak as Ken was talking. "Kitten, I know this is soon, but I love you. I've loved you from the very moment I saw you. And it wasn't your legs that captivated my heart, although I'll admit they got my attention. It's your innocence, your meekness, I find so alluring.

"But I have to tell you that it was your legs that made this huge diamond possible. I was paid handsomely for the ad, and I never did pay you for your part in it. I figured you deserved a gorgeous diamond.

"Please tell me that you'll be my wife. So many exciting things have been happening to me since this ad came out. It means big money. I want you to be a part of it all, a part of my life. What do you say, Kitten?"

"Oh. Oh my," was all she could manage.

"You do love me, don't you?"

"Y-yes . . . this . . . so fast."

"If you love me, that's all I need to know. We'll worry about the rest at some later time. For now, I give this ring to my wife-to-be." He placed the ring on her finger, then sealed it with a kiss.

Ken and Katie finished the bottle of champagne, then left the restaurant and went to his apartment. Katie realized when she entered the door that this evening might have one more surprise for her. But somehow she didn't care. The huge diamond ring and the champagne had caused a strange pulsation between her legs, a yearning inside that needed filled.

"I'll be gentle," said Ken. "I know this is your first time." His hot lips kissed her over and over again. Then he spread her legs, and kissed her some more.

When they finished, for some reason, her mother's statement about a rooster's tail popped into Katie's head. "I don't know what you meant about a rooster's tail spoiling the soup, Mama," she thought, "but this sure was good soup tonight."

It was time for Ken to take Katie home. She could have stayed all night, but thinking about the rooster tail sparked a responsibility within her. Her mother would worry about her. She must get home.

When she awoke the next morning, she thought she had dreamed it all. But there was the ring in the box on the nightstand where she had placed it. And there was a soiled pair of panties lying on the floor.

She picked up the soiled panties and smelled them. It made something twitch within her, something that twitched too much last night.

She looked out the window and saw the huge maple shooting its first chestnut colors of spring. "I just hope he doesn't want to rush this marriage thing," she thought. She wanted at least to complete college, get a degree in psychology, and make something of herself. Marriages took a long time to plan. Maybe they could go on for years like this, like last night.

"Oh, no!" she said to herself. He obviously hadn't used any protection—otherwise her panties wouldn't be so soiled. Next time, they'd have to be more careful. Maybe she could get some of those birth control pills she'd been hearing about.

The telephone rang. "Katie, it's for you. It's Ken."

"Thanks, Mother. I'll be right down." She put on her robe and ran downstairs.

"Hello, Kitten. Did you sleep well?"

"Yes. Maybe too long. What time is it anyway?"

"Last night was the happiest of my life. What does your mother think about your ring?"

"To tell you the truth, she doesn't know about it yet. I just got up. How about you? Have you told your family yet?"

He didn't answer her question. "I was wondering if we could meet for lunch. Nothing fancy. Just a hamburger and coke, fast food. I have something else I want to talk with you about."

"Something else? Sure." Katie couldn't imagine what that might be. After all, she had yet to process the events from last evening. Now Ken had more rain to pour on her brain. She felt flooded, light-headed.

Since she was underage, she'd undoubtedly have to get her mother's approval before they could marry. But she wanted her advice as well.

Before she hung up the phone, she heard a car start. She looked at the clock. It was 8:30. On a Sunday morning, that would be her mother leaving for church. Their much-needed talk would have to wait until later in the day.

At lunch Ken told her that Tyson Foods, a huge company in Arkansas, had approached him with a job offer. "They want me to handle all their advertising. They've offered me an incredibly lucrative contract with a huge sign-on bonus. Think of this Kitten! With that money I can purchase my own advertising agency. I won't have to work for jerks anymore. And we'll still have enough to buy a nice home."

"Tyson Foods? Arkansas? What would that mean to us?" Katie asked, worriedly.

Ken didn't seem to hear her questions, but sped ahead. "The only drawback is, they need my answer within two weeks."

"Two weeks? That doesn't seem like much time to decide an important lifetime decision. What would that mean for us?"

"It means if I took the job, we'd have to move to Little Rock shortly thereafter. Within a month."

Katie gasped. Her mother didn't even know she was engaged. And now, they'd be moving away!

"What do you think? Kitten. Could we put together a wedding, say, in a week?"

"I haven't talked with my mother about this. I'm under twenty-one, you know. She'll have to sign for me."

"The law was changed a couple of years ago to eighteen, so you won't need your mother's approval. I'm sure we can get married within a month. I'll work it all out for us."

Katie wanted to say, "Wait! This is moving much too fast for me. Let's slow down. I have to finish college." But before she could get the words up from her throat and into her mouth, Ken had more words.

"I'll telephone Tyson tomorrow and accept their offer."

It seemed to Katie that Ken's words came into his mouth as easily as spit, while hers must be dredged from her core. Yet when she spoke, they meant no more than the wraps and napkins hurriedly tossed into the trash bin as they exited the hamburger joint.

She barely remembered the drive to her home, his "Call you tomorrow" punctuated with a kiss.

But then the reminder on Monday. "Hi Kitten! Guess what? I've made the arrangements. We can get our blood tests on Friday of this week. Then we'll get our marriage license. I've talked with Tyson Foods, told them I'll take their offer. Did you tell your mother yet? What did she say about us getting married?"

"She thought the ring was beautiful, Ken."

She and her mother had talked about much more, conversations she felt uneasy sharing with Ken. For instance, Katie didn't tell him that her mother was not one to be dazzled by diamonds. Their rushed courtship and marriage concerned her. She reminded Katie of the old adage, "Marry in haste, repent in leisure" and advised her to take it to heart.

She further stated, "Katharina, you are the first of my children to graduate from high school. And now you're attending college. Your older brothers and sisters weren't so lucky."

"I know I've been fortunate, Mother."

"It's natural for a girl your age to want to get married, but I would advise you to get your education first. Make something of your life. Put something in your brain. If things get tough, you'll always be able to fall back on what's in your head and make a decent living for yourself and any children you might have."

"But Mother, I plan to continue my education. I'll still be able to go to college in Arkansas."

"In Arkansas?"

"Oh, yes, Ken has accepted a huge ad contract with Tyson Foods. He must be in Little Rock in a month."

"That means you'll be getting married soon."

"Yes, Mother, I will have to make some fast plans. Naturally, I want you, my brothers and sisters there. And I thought I would ask Sue to be my maid-of-honor. And then I'll ask my sisters to be my bridesmaids."

"Your best friend Sue is a good choice for maid-of-honor. But all five of your sisters as bridesmaids?"

"No, I guess I better just have the two that aren't married yet, but then . . . oh dear, Ken has one sister and I should ask her to be one also. Well, three isn't too many. Ken has one brother. I'm sure he'll definitely want him to be best man. And I want some of my brothers in the wedding party also. And then there is Joe. Joe has been so helpful to me since we moved to Pittsburgh. I love him like a brother."

"Katharina, before you go making wedding plans, tell me, are you sure this is the man you want to spend the rest of your life with?"

"I'm very much in love with him, Mother. Yes, I'm sure."

"Then I'll do my best to help you plan a nice wedding. I just would like for it to be in a church. You don't attend my church, but I'm sure you could have it there in the chapel. It's nice. Maybe Ken goes to church. Or his parents. Do you know whether they do?"

"I don't know," Katie stammered. "I haven't met his parents or his brother or sister yet. I'll ask Ken about it today."

Ken did *not* want to get married in a church, but at the LeMont Restaurant. For sentimental reasons, he said. After all, that was where he had given her the ring. And further, he was surprised she'd even suggest another place.

He informed her he checked and found the place would be available for a Saturday night in four weeks. He put a tentative hold on that date until he talked with his bride-to-be. An overwhelmed Katie found herself going along.

He itemized his suggestions for their wedding: small, informal, no more than fifty people, a maid-of-honor, a best man, family, closest friends. "We'll hire a photographer for some nice wedding pictures.

"After the wedding, we'll have champagne toasts and hors d'oeuvres. We'll treat our guests to a sit-down dinner. We'll hire a nice three-piece ensemble for dancing, then top off the night in the honeymoon suite at the William Penn hotel. The following morning we'll leave for Arkansas."

"But I . . ." Katie finally got some words into her mouth, only to have them left hanging like clothes in the wind.

"But you wanted a large wedding party, didn't you? I know that's what you were going to say. Believe me, Kitten, I would want it that way too if we had more time, but we don't. It'll be so much less stress for you if we keep it simple." And he kissed her so tenderly that her brain sent no more words to her mouth.

Katie didn't have to work Monday or Tuesday. On Wednesday, as soon as she got to Klein's Seafood, she showed

Jenny her diamond and told her about her wedding plans and the move to Arkansas. Jenny looked shocked.

"Jenny, aren't you happy for me?"

"I've come to care for you deeply, even though we haven't known each other long. Actually, just two short months. Dear Katie, you've got feathers in your eyes. You're not thinking anymore. Getting married in a month, then moving to Arkansas. I've been around a little longer than you. Meet me in the bathroom."

"Now?"

"Yes, now! Some things are so important, you have to put everything else aside."

"But we'll have to hurry. There's no one to cover these tables."

"It won't take long. Just come!"

When they got to the bathroom, Jenny undid the front of her uniform, then pulled her breasts out of her bra. "Look at this! Scars! Ugly scars from cigarette burns!"

Katie gasped. "Why! How!"

"My ex! My ex did this! Tied me down, then did this. Believe me, that was the last night I saw him! I just want you to know that things like this can occur if you don't know exactly what you're getting into."

Katie gulped. She was unaware that things like this ever took place.

"Ruined me for life. That's why I say: Don't jump into a marriage too soon! Live with him. Do anything. Just don't marry him yet. Once you marry a man, he thinks you're his property."

"Oh, the mad dog thing. I remember now. You said something about knowing a mad dog when you saw one. You were saying that because of what your ex did to you. Why are you saying this to me?"

"Because Ken gives me those feelings. Why do you think I'm going to all this trouble? Do you think I show my burned boobs to everyone?"

"Oh, Jen, I'm terribly sorry about what happened to you, but what you think about Ken is incorrect. He's never asked me for anything other than a kiss, never until last Saturday that is. And that was to celebrate our engagement, and I can honestly say that was as much my fault as his. I can tell you he has never been anything other than a perfect gentleman. No, Jenny, I don't worry at all about how Ken will treat me."

"You've only known him for how long? Not even two months? How can you know him?"

"I know this is a little fast. I also wish we could slow it down. But he has to go where the opportunities are. And an exceptional opportunity has knocked at his door. One he wants to share with me. I think that's commendable."

They were interrupted by a pounding on the bathroom door. "Customers are waiting."

"We're coming," said Katie. Then she said to Jen, "It's really nice of you to be so concerned about me, but I'll be all right. You'll see. You'll come to my wedding, won't you?"

"Sure, Katie, and I really do wish you the best. Nevertheless, I can't help worrying about you."

"After I move to Arkansas, promise me one thing. Promise me you'll come to visit. Then I'll show you how fine things really are between Ken and me. I'll even show you my boobs so that you can see I'm okay." She gave Jenny a big hug.

Jenny hugged her back. "I hope things work out for you. And you don't have to show me your boobs. I've been around enough to know that not all scars are on the skin. Some scars are within, like scarred hearts, scarred spirits. But we better get to work before we're fired."

***

Katie wanted to have some definite information regarding a proposed meeting before answering Frank's letter. At last she had a time.

Ken preferred—insisted, in fact—that she travel to Pittsburgh to visit her family when he was away on business. He had a seminar scheduled the second week of July.

Katie checked with her mother. "Sure, Katharina. That time will be fine, wonderful. I've contacted your brothers and sisters and it will be good for them as well. We'll be delighted to see you."

Katie was ready to write to Frank. She could have told him how her spirit longed for the kindness and tenderness he conveyed in his letters, how his words provided a nutrient she lacked in her life, a requirement she needed anymore just to make it through the day. But she kept this to herself and focused on the real purpose of their association, and answered professionally.

> Dear Frank,
>
> You can't imagine how much I enjoyed the story of Hans Reyher. You delight and amuse me by writing it in fiction. I think writing fiction is fun and freeing. Did you feel that way when you were doing it?
>
> I have so much admiration and respect for Hans in deciding to leave his homeland and family. It must have been heart-wrenching for him to say good-bye to a world of love and knowns, and face a future of unknowns. But he was willing to choose the unknown perils of freedom rather than the known hardships of what for him was an oppressive system: primogeniture.
>
> From the little that you have told me about our great-great-grandfather, Johann Gotthard, it seems that he followed a similar path. Didn't he also leave the comforts of his hometown and family to escape an oppressive system, the mercenary system, where boys his age were rented out by his government to foreign armies? Would not the obstacles and unknown perils in his decision to emigrate to the United States require great fortitude?

*Again I have to thank you and your mother for all the work you have done in uncovering our family's rich heritage. Until our correspondence began, I hadn't even known that the fellow I called John had emigrated from Germany. I guess people never know these things without a resourceful family member (or members in your case) willing to dig into past documents and unearth genealogy gems.*

*Please continue to relay to me your ideas regarding fate and chance. I find them refreshingly thought-provoking. Our paths did cross in a most unusual way. Our respective time and space dimensions did intersect at a common point, but I'm not so sure about "readiness." Can it be defined in terms of a point? For me, readiness has a subjective quality that is dependent upon the individual's state of mind, whereas time and space are objective qualities. What do you think?*

*You asked me about the possibility of our getting together in Pittsburgh rather than Columbiana to discuss OUR book project in depth. I am happy to tell you that I'll be able to do so.*

*My husband doesn't like for me to travel when he's home so I usually try to visit my family in Pittsburgh when he's on a business trip. He has one planned for the middle of July. I have called my mother and she says it is convenient for her, as well as for my brothers and sisters, if I visit them that week—from July 14 through 21, to be precise.*

*If you can meet me in Pittsburgh sometime during that week, I'll gladly make arrangements on whatever day suits you best. I'll have use of my mother's car, so I can meet you anywhere. I'll leave the selection of a suitable place up to you. If you want to, we can wait to select a place after I get to Pittsburgh. I'll give you my mother's telephone number and you can call me there.*

*I am anxiously looking forward to mid-July.*
*With warm regards,*
*Katie*

# 7

## COMING TO AMERICA

Frank could scarcely contain his excitement as he read Katie's letter. Finally, he was going to meet her—and in just a couple of weeks!

He checked his calendar and noted he'd be off the sixteenth and the twentieth. He chose the earlier date.

Where should they meet? If he took I-76 from Youngstown to Pittsburgh, it would take an hour and half at the most. He could leave in the morning and be there before noon.

Not wishing to take a chance that something might go awry, he decided to inform Katie immediately about his available day. But should he send her some more of his creative writing? As Katie said, writing fiction was fun, although her comment about it being freeing left him perplexed. Regardless, after writing the Hans Reyher story, he had found it impossible to "put down his pen." He now was near the end of Johann Gotthard's story.

Frank noticed that Katie emphasized the word *our* when talking about the book project. This meant she definitely planned to collaborate on a book with him. Why shouldn't he share the Johann story? After all, she asked questions about Johann and, quite validly, compared the two flights from oppression.

Frank had the following day off and spent it polishing

Johann's story. Finally, he was ready to answer Katie's e-mail.

> Dear Katie,
> 
> I can't tell you how much your e-mails mean to me. I used to spend long hours at my office, hating to return to my empty home. Now I find myself leaving as early as possible in the hope I will find correspondence from you. Your letters are delightful! You have brought untold happiness into my life.
> 
> I know it sounds trite, but my heart skipped a beat when you told me you could meet me in Pittsburgh in a couple of weeks. I have looked at my calendar and am free on the sixteenth. It will be a short zip for me from Youngstown over to Pittsburgh. I thought we could meet for lunch—nothing fancy—but somewhere that has good food and a quiet corner. I will telephone you at your mother's. I'm sure you will send me her telephone number shortly so I can reach you.
> 
> When I read your stories from childhood, I can envisage how difficult life must have been for you at times. By comparison my background seems secure and ordinary. I guess I was spoiled. It is my impression, though, that creative people like yourself always seem to make the most of the difficulties in their lives.
> 
> Your reaction to what I wrote about Hans was most encouraging. I found it interesting that you were amused at my attempts to write fiction. To be honest with you, I chuckled from time to time too as I attempted to fictionalize our ancestors' lives. At any rate, I'm glad I can bring laughter into your life.
> 
> I used the plural of ancestor in the above paragraph, because, as you will see, I couldn't just stop with Hans. I have been writing about Johann, fictionalizing his story

as well, which I'll share with you too. As you surmised, the two stories have common elements.

I'm glad to have your comments regarding fate, chance, and the crossing of paths. You bring up an interesting point. Readiness may indeed be a subjective quality.

It has occurred to me that modern technology greatly increases the likelihood of paths crossing. Look at how commercial jets bring us closer together. Look at the opportunities created by home computers, by the Internet, by genealogy software. These new tools and media clearly help to bring people together. Still, we don't have an answer to the basic question: What dominates, fate or chance?

After sending you Hans' story, I have focused on Johann Gotthard's departure for, and subsequent early years in, the U.S. For the past week I have filled my evenings working on a fictionalized story of that episode as well, and finished it just last evening. The story is dying to get out of my computer and into your hands.

As I did before, I'll send it as an attachment to this e-mail. You'll note I'm entitling it "Flight of the Heron II." I should have entitled the Hans' story "Flight of the Heron I." I had no idea I'd get so hooked on fiction that I'd be writing a sequel a few days later! I'll continue this letter in a separate e-mail, lest this one get too long.

I'm sure you'll find the section on Katharina (your name-sake) particularly interesting.

\*\*\*

ATTACHMENT

## *Flight of the Heron II*

The prized grandfather clock struck ten, and it was quiet at last. Johann Gotthard, twenty, oldest of the nine surviving

Reyher children, and his sister Christina, seventeen, were out visiting friends. All of the other children were in bed.

"What are we going to do about Gotthard?" Anna asked her husband, Johann Melchior Reyher. The couple had named three of their sons Johann, and, to avoid confusion, now referred to them by their middle names.

Johann looked up from the notes he was making at the desk and sighed. "I don't know. He's always so critical of everything. Sure, times have been tough here in Wuerttemberg, but they seem to be getting better finally."

Anna knew her husband was alluding to the harvest failure a couple of years earlier that had shocked the authorities to the point of at last taking steps to create a significant grain reserve. And that program, in turn, had helped to buttress the prices they received for their crops. "But," she said, "it's not so much the economic situation that Gotthard criticizes as those 'scoundrels in Stuttgart,' as he puts it."

"Yes," Johann agreed. "And he can't seem to stop swooning over America. He's been talking about a new Promised Land ever since he's gotten to know that zany geography teacher, Herr Wildermuth."

"That's just the fantasizing of young people," Anna said. "We did it too when we were Gotthard's age. What bothers me more is how Gotthard might be reacting to those letters from the Ulmer boy in Pennsylvania. His parents know how Gotthard always idolized Georg, so they think they're doing him a favor by letting him see their son's letters."

"I've got to admit," Johann said, "when I hear of the possibility of getting a hundred sixty acres of land for virtually nothing, I sometimes long to be twenty years younger."

"I know," responded Anna. "You've always had a wild streak in you too."

Just then Gotthard came in, looking very glum.

"You won't believe what I just heard," he told his parents.

"Maybe not," his mother said wearily, "but tell us anyhow."

"Those bastards in Stuttgart have dreamed up a new way of filling the state's coffers. Like the prince of Hessia, they are going to sell mercenary services to the British. Only we Swabians, instead of fighting American revolutionaries, get to pacify the Indians—the ones in south Asia, that is."

Johann and Anna normally had little stomach for Gotthard's fulminations, which usually involved people or events far removed from the familiar Pleidelsheim scene. This time, though, they exchanged worried looks. The report Gotthard had picked up somehow had a ring of truth to it. Since the King was in the process of making his monarchy constitutional, he could no longer levy new taxes arbitrarily. Parliament had to approve them, but probably wouldn't, given the trend everywhere in post-Congress of Vienna Europe toward armed forces demobilization and tax reduction.

When it came to the Wuerttemberg army, however, the King's rule was still absolute, for all intents and purposes. Not only was he commander-in-chief, but current law gave him the right to draft any male subject between eighteen and twenty-five and to expand and deploy the army at will, so long as he did not have to go back to Parliament for more money. So he could make a simple business deal, which could be summarized as follows:

Revenues—i.e., what the British were willing to pay—minus costs—i.e., the pittance that was paid the draftees—equaled profit—i.e., the moneys the king could keep or use as he saw fit.

"Oh my God," Johann finally said. "I never dreamed the man would stoop that low."

"Maybe the new constitution will prohibit it," Anna said.

"Don't count on it, mother," Gotthard said. "But even if it did, remember, the new constitution still hasn't been promulgated. In the interim the King is free to make his mercenary deals. And I'm a prime candidate for his delightful army."

Anna looked at her son and fought back tears. What mother ever found it easy to accept the drafting of a son, especially her first-born, into the army? If the army was defending their country, there would at least be a suitable rationale. But drafting young men to fight in some other sovereign's foreign war? That was abominable. She felt helpless and very tired. "I'm going to bed," was all she could say.

The months passed by. The Reyhers, busy with the harvest, did not discuss the painful subject again. It was almost as if they made a pact to avoid it. In fact, Johann and Anna independently noticed that Gotthard had become uncharacteristically reserved in his comments about political developments and issues in general, but they did not discuss that subject either. They both realized that there were things about their son they did not understand, but also that they had no way of inducing him to share his thoughts with them.

On April 15, 1819, the following notice appeared on the bulletin board at the Rathaus:

### Notice to 20-Year-Old Men

All men who will have reached their 20th birthday between May 1, 1818, and April 30, 1819, are to appear at the army regional headquarters in Marbach a.N. on or before May 15 for the purpose of undergoing a physical examination to determine their suitability for induction into the Wuerttemberg army.

The only men exempted from this requirement are those certified by the appropriate authority to:
1) have an incurable communicative disease,
2) be employed in an occupation deemed essential by the state, or,

3) be the only surviving son in a family in which at least one of the parents is still living.

Inductees will serve in the army for a period of three years. Under extraordinary circumstances, this period can be extended for an additional two years by H.M. the King, provided he communicates the reasons for such extension in writing to Parliament.

Initial remuneration for the inductees is set at Level 1 of the Civil Service pay schedule. Annual increases are granted for satisfactory performance. Promotions to higher pay levels and even commissioning as officers are possible.

Within hours all the affected young men in Pleidelsheim were informed.

"Annual increases for satisfactory performance," Gotthard muttered to his friend, Gilbert Wildermuth, who alerted him to the notice. "A ten percent increase over the current Level 1 would still be a starvation wage. But, then we shouldn't forget the extra benefits: You get to put your life on line for British control of India."

Later, that evening, Johann asked his son, "Did you see the notice at the Rathaus?"

"Yes father," Gotthard answered.

"Is that all you have to say?"

"What can I say? We knew this was coming."

"What will you do?"

"As you have often said, Father, 'the law is the law.'"

Johann saw that he was not going to draw out his son this time either. Anna, who heard the exchange, just shook her head and sighed.

It was just after midnight, May 6. The last drunkard had gone home from the "Stern" pub. Gotthard and Gilbert had been there too, as they had been for the past several evenings, drinking much more than usual and staying until the pub closed. Everyone assumed this was Gotthard's way of enjoying his last few days of freedom before being drafted. So tonight was no different, except that this time Gotthard and Gilbert had surreptitiously dumped most of their beer out the window and thus only feigned their boisterous highs.

Outside, Gotthard and Gilbert intentionally said a loud good-night to each other, should a sleepless neighbor happen to be listening. Then, whispering occasionally, they headed down Gross-Ingersheimer Strasse for the Neckar landing dock where several small boats were tied. They boarded one of them, and Gilbert silently rowed his friend around the island to the other shore and docked behind a bush. They got out and embraced.

"Gilbert, I will never be able to thank you for this," Gotthard said, still whispering.

Gilbert smiled. "My reward comes from knowing you have thumbed your nose at 'His Majesty.'"

"I'm very worried about my family."

"I can't tell you not to worry, because I know you will," Gilbert said. "But you were quite right not to tell them in advance, and your plan is a good one."

"I hope you're right," said Gotthard. "Good-bye, my friend. You'll hear from me."

"Godspeed, Gotthard." Gilbert got into the boat and rowed back to the Pleidelsheim side of the Neckar. The last thing he did was throw Gotthard's favorite jacket into the river and push the boat away from the dock. Both objects floated in the rapidly-moving water, eventually to become snagged or run aground somewhere downstream.

Gotthard headed to the west, carefully skirting nearby Ingersheim. He passed to the north of Bietigheim and reached the Enz, a tributary of the Neckar, which, fortunately, was narrow enough that there were several foot bridges in the area. He crossed one of them and headed into the hills, where he could breathe a bit easier. He wanted to cover at least ten miles before daybreak, when he would rest in an appropriately secluded area.

Gotthard knew as long as he was in Wuerttemberg, he must be extremely careful. His disappearance from Pleidelsheim would be immediately noticed, but he was not so sure that people would fall for his ruse drowning. "Where is the body?" they would ask.

In any case, the authorities in Marbach could be counted on to be suspicious about the circumstances of his disappearance and to put out an 1819-style all-points bulletin. The King's henchmen realized that their hated draft would work only if they were widely perceived to be relentless and rigorous in pursuing "conscientious objectors." That was why they instituted check-points along all waterways and coach roads in the Kingdom. The great majority of escapees would try no other route, because they were terrified of the hill country, which was popularly regarded as full of all types of supernatural as well as natural perils.

Gotthard was carrying only a few pounds, packed in an old but warm blanket that Gilbert had given him. Much of the weight consisted of imperishable food. At all costs he must avoid getting caught pilfering farmers' produce while he was still in Wuerttemberg. He carried only one extra shirt and pair of socks. Even though he realized he would quickly begin to look—and smell—like a vagabond, he had no choice.

Once he was safely out of the Kingdom, he might consider buying cheap second-hand clothes, but only after he was sure his meager savings would get him to Amsterdam. Taking anything from his parents would have undercut the story he wanted them to believe: that he drowned while trying to get to the pub across the river in Ingersheim, which often stayed open longer than either the Stern or the Ochsen.

Following the Kirchbach stream up a ravine, Gotthard made reasonably good time. The decision to escape when the moon was almost full paid off. Visibility was no problem, except in wooded areas. Luckily, the weather cooperated in another way too. It was warm enough for him to get by with his one blanket. Just outside of Spielberg he found a sheltered spot where he could sleep much of the next day.

After two nights of hard walking, Gotthard reached the edge of the Rhine valley near Karlsruhe. Although he knew he was practically out of the authorities' reach now, he did not want to take chances by boarding a Rhine boat in such a big town. So he continued his marathon walk a third night and finally caught a Dutch boat at Germersheim. Gotthard figured, correctly, that its skipper would be quite unconcerned about the *bona-fides* of any particular vagabond so long as he was able to pay hard cash for the passage.

Ten days later, the boat deposited Gotthard at a landing on the lower Rhine near Utrecht. From there he was able to get a coach to Amsterdam. On June 1 he arrived in the city, then as now one of the great metropolises of Europe. Just a little more than three weeks after leaving Pleidelsheim, the normally agnostic Gotthard said a little prayer of thanks for his safe arrival.

Then he went to a public scribe and had him send a postcard to Gilbert with the following message: "There are seagulls everywhere here in Amsterdam. You would love the city." As the two friends had agreed, Gilbert would know this message meant: "I arrived safely in Amsterdam, but there are many people waiting for passage."

No one in the provincial Pleidelsheim would suspect anything, because, after all, Gilbert corresponded with people all over the place. In fact, they would be happy for him, since receiving mail was always exciting, and they knew Gilbert had been very depressed, blaming himself for the loss of his friend Gotthard in the drowning incident.

Upon receipt of the card, Gilbert called on the Reyhers and told them, in great confidence, that their son was alive, well, and on his way to America. He would withhold any details until he knew Gotthard had safely arrived at his final destination.

Gotthard quickly found out that his hope of earning money to pay for his passage to the U.S. was ill-founded. While odd jobs were available everywhere in Amsterdam, the pay was barely enough to cover his room and board. Gotthard was forced to consider alternatives.

There were plenty of ships available, summer being the peak season, and Gotthard was able to meet with one captain after another. The problem was most of them insisted on full payment in advance. That would have taken Gotthard years to accumulate.

Unless he "sold his soul" for passage.

During the 18th century, Gotthard learned, many emigrants to America, especially out of British ports, did not pay a penny out of their own pockets for the passage. Instead, before departing for the New World each signed an indenture agreement with an agent who represented an American interested in buying labor services for a stipulated period. The agent then paid the captain for the emigrant's passage and ultimately collected the amount that the buyer in America had agreed to pay. Naturally, this normally would be substantially more than the cost of passage, thus ensuring a tidy profit for the agent.

Often the agent had no specific buyer for the services, but, being familiar with the American labor market, speculated on being able eventually to sell the indenture contract for an even greater profit. In any case, the emigrant was legally bound to work for the owner of the indenture during the period specified in the agreement. The average period was four years. Such was the system at one time.

By 1819, however, the institution of indentured servitude as practiced in the 18th century had become relatively rare in the U.S. What still was employed occasionally was the "redemptioner system." Under this system, the emigrant paid whatever he could of the cost of his passage before leaving Europe and promised to pay the balance when he arrived in the New World.

Upon arrival, the emigrant had up to two weeks to meet his obligation. If he was fortunate enough to have generous relatives or friends in the U.S. to help, he did. If not (which often happened), he had to sign an indenture agreement. The period of servitude varied depending on how much partial payment, if any, he had made, and on his value as perceived by those buying his services.

A ship captain, to whom the emigrant gave a formal IOU with an indenture clause, knew exactly *what* he would be paid: the cost of passage. *Whether* he would be paid was uncertain, of course. For instance, the captain had no recourse if the emigrant died en route, which still happened, though much less frequently than it once did. He also might lose his money if, upon arrival in the U.S., the emigrant simply disappeared. This rarely happened, however, since the U.S. justice system in those days was rather efficient in tracking down and punishing errant debtors. Faced with these possibilities, most captains developed a keen sense of judgment as to which emigrants would survive the passage and pay off their obligations.

One such captain was John Welsh, who, when Gotthard spoke with him in Amsterdam, quickly decided that the Swabian was a man he could trust. He had Gotthard sign the requisite IOU for exactly $42.30, the cost of passage—padded a bit, of course, to give Welsh some extra profit for his residual risk.

Gotthard knew he would not find anyone in the New World to pay this amount for him and thus would have to sign an indenture agreement. What he did *not* know was the length of his prospective period of servitude.

Under the redemptioner system, it was the *emigrant* who bore the biggest risk. If Gotthard arrived in a weakened condition as a result of sickness, his value to a buyer would go down and the period of his servitude would lengthen. In addition, as in any commodity market, the value of indentures rose and fell depending on supply and demand. Thus, even if Gotthard were in top shape, the price for his indenture might command a year or two of his life longer than he had expected!

Welsh's ship, the Brigadier Osgood, sailed on August 20. After a difficult passage (as all were in those days), the ship arrived in Philadelphia on September 27. Two days later, Johann Gotthard Reyher, no doubt after considerable agonizing over the direction the labor market might take, decided to end the uncertainty. He signed the following agreement:

### *This Indenture*

WITNESSETH, That Johann Gotthart Reyher, with consent [i.e., in the presence] of Daniel Libo, has bound himself Servant to John Buckholder of Canastoga [sic] Township, Lancaster County, farmer, for the consideration of Forty-three 20/100 dollars paid to John Welsh for his passage from Amsterdam.

As also for other good causes he, the said Johann Gotthart Reyher, hath bound and put himself and by these Presents doth bind and put himself Servant to the said John Buckholder to serve him, his Executors, Administrators and Assigns from the day of the date hereof, for and during the full term of Three years from thence ensuing. During all which term the said Servant his master, his Executors, Administrators and Assigns faithfully shall serve, and that honestly and obediently in all things, as a good and faithful Servant ought to do. And the said John Buckholder, his Executors, Administrators and Assigns, during the said term shall find and provide for the said Servant sufficient Meat, Drink, Apparel, Washing and

Lodging and six weeks schooling. And at the end of the term give him two complete suits of clothes, one of which to be new, or pay him Thirty-five 80/100 dollars.

And for the true performance hereof, both the said parties bind themselves firmly unto each other by these Presents. In Witness whereof they have interchangeably set their Hands and Seals. Dated the twenty-ninth day of September A.D., one thousand eight hundred and nineteen.

Bound before
[signed by Conrad Wile, Registrar]
[signed by Johann Gottfried Reyher]
[signed by Daniel Libo]

Thus Gotthard locked in a three-year period, thankful it was not four or more. It is a mystery why Gotthard signed his middle name "Gottfried" whereas elsewhere in the indenture agreement the name "Gotthart" was clearly legible. The most likely explanation is that he had assumed no one would be able to read his signature in old German script, which was certainly true. However, if comparisons were made, it was desirable that the signature be identical to that on the IOU he had given Captain Welsh before leaving Amsterdam. Welsh's records, according to the National Archives, in fact indicated the name of his passenger as "Johann Gottfried Reyher."

In Amsterdam Gotthard probably worried about the long arm of the Wuerttemberg law and reasoned that the name Gottfried, which was not found in his family, would lead any investigators astray. In the New World he could safely become Gotthard again.

In any case, Gotthard gave up his freedom for the next three years in the U.S. Fortunately for him, indentured servitude, having become relatively rare, was no longer as widely abused as it had been during the colonial period. John

Buckholder was probably aware that he would find little legal support for problems arising out of any mistreatment of Gotthard, so he treated him well. And the young German, as he served his time, learned the ways and the language of his adopted country. He was lonely, of course, but the same iron determination that had enabled him to slip out of Pleidelsheim undetected got him through this difficult period as well.

As fate would have it, the Buckholders moved from Pennsylvania to eastern Ohio during Gotthard's servitude. It was there that his period of indentureship ended, rendering John Reyher, as he now called himself, free at last to do as he pleased.

With his "meat, drink, apparel, washing and lodging" no longer provided, John now had to earn a living for himself. Farming was what he knew, so he became a farm hand, working for various employers, sometimes two or three at the same time.

His hard work and honesty made him popular among potential employers, especially those who still spoke German. One of them was Elias Friedrich Wilhelm, known in the New World as Frederick Wilhelm.

Frederick had emigrated to the U.S. in 1804 with his wife and five surviving children. Their home town had been Oelbronn, in Wuerttemberg, just twenty miles to the west of Pleidelsheim.

Very well off compared with most immigrants, Frederick soon bought a one-hundred thirty-nine acre farm in Fairfield Township of Columbiana County. It was a good place to live and to raise his children. He doted especially over his only daughter, Katharina Wilhelm, who became known as Catherine in the U.S. She was just three when they had emigrated and therefore became the most Americanized of his European-born children.

Frederick did not mind when his daughter refused to speak German and corrected his English. But he did think that she would be better off marrying a solid German rather than one of those lazy Americans who were showing a lot of interest in her.

In 1822, when he was fifty-nine, Frederick promised his farm to Catherine as a way of getting her commitment to taking care of him and his wife in their old age. To make such a gift possible, Frederick that year bought another, even larger farm (one-hundred-fifty-eight acres) in Green Township through the Steubenville land office. Five years later, he divided it into separate but equal plots for his two oldest sons, Christian Friedrich "Frederick Jr." and Johann Jakob "Jacob." Obviously still influenced by the principle of primogeniture, Frederick failed to provide land to any of his three youngest sons, Johannes, Gottlieb, and his only American-born child, David. That omission made his promise to Catherine, his second-youngest child, all the more remarkable.

No one knew exactly when Catherine met John Reyher. Their paths conceivably could have crossed even before John completed his indentureship at the end of September 1822, since by then they both lived in the same general area. According to prevailing family lore, John found work as a farm hand and met Catherine at the Wilhelms sometime in 1823.

Frederick liked John's industriousness and discipline, not to mention his ability and willingness to joke and chat in the Swabian dialect. On the negative side, Frederick rued John's lowly status: As a recent indentured servant, he was anything but the social equal of a Wilhelm. Frederick finally accepted John as his future son-in-law when Catherine, by then going on twenty-five, started complaining about being called an "old maid." The two were married in early 1826, about three years after they met. Their first child, Elias, was born on November 10 of that year.

Frederick formally sold the original Wilhelm farm, as it was to be called for generations thereafter, to his daughter Catherine and son-in-law John Reyher for $1,600 in 1831. The young couple had been working the farm for several years, even before they got married. The price paid represented the value of the sixty acres that Catherine had received in excess of the seventy-nine-acre plots given to Frederick Jr. and Jacob.

John never actually paid $1,600 to Frederick. Rather, the two came to regard the amount as a kind of supplemental dowry, in effect a way of encouraging John to honor his wife's commitment of old-age care, a matter of increasing importance to Frederick, now sixty-eight.

In any case, John would not have been able to pay cash, as his financial problems following the indentureship were not solved by the marriage. In fact, family records include an attestation dated August 22, 1827, from the supervisor of Beaver Township indicating that John had performed labor on public roads in order to pay just $0.11 in taxes he owed!

While by no means rich, John had clearly come a long ways in the eleven long years after leaving Pleidelsheim. His growing sense of security induced him, in 1832, to bring over his younger brother, Peter ("Johann Peter"), to help on the farm. In 1834, his parents, by then fifty-nine and fifty-seven years old, joined them. What had been a Reyher dynasty in Pleidelsheim was fast becoming a Reyher dynasty in eastern Ohio. Nevertheless, John was hesitant to cut his ties to the Old World. It was 1842 before he was finally naturalized as a U.S. citizen.

***

(New e-mail, continuing where the other left off)
> *I am sure, Katie, that you will want to add some dialog "meat" to the "bones" of my story. I've provided the basic facts, which I can document. In fact, seeing the indenture agreement and realizing that our ancestor actually signed it sent chills down my back. Imagine, three years of your life for $43!*

My life has been reinvigorated by my wonderful trip to Pleidelsheim and by the stories I have been sharing with you about our ancestors. In fact, this whole correspondence of ours, and the idea of a visit to the past through a book collaboration, have revived my spirit in ways that I can hardly convey to you.

I thought about telling you this in earlier correspondence, but it was still so raw within me that I have had difficulty putting it into words. I feel I can do so now. My wife Sally died in a car accident about eighteen months ago. My difficulty in getting on with my life was the reason I took up genealogy.

You mentioned in your first letter to me that you had concerns about leaving the farmhouse where you were born and which you shared with your father until his death. You said you were afraid you would forget your father without familiar surrounding objects to bring his memories alive.

To be honest with you, I've had these same fears since Sally's death. I have been afraid to get rid of things that remind me of her, lest I get rid of her memories as well. As you so poignantly describe, we have these memories in our head. Our sense stimuli are not limited either by time or location, but can trigger memories no matter where we are.

When Sally died, a bit of me died too. Or so I thought until now. Nothing I did, be it at work or in my off hours, seemed to get me back to where I had been. That's different now. Thank you, Katie, for coming into my life as an e-mail correspondent.

And now I'll soon meet you. I am looking forward to hearing your voice live, to testing my imagination against reality. I can't tell you how much I anticipate that occasion.
Fondly,
Frank
P.S. I'm sure you will readily note that the Wilheim Farm is the same one on which you were born.

# 8

## THE WEDDING

Katie finished reading Frank's e-mail and attachment, then placed it on the table before her. The ancestral information should have filled her with joy. However, she barely gave it a second thought, and focused instead on Frank's personal letter.

Was she crazy, having agreed to meet with him? Her earlier fantasies about running through pastures with him, and playing peek-a-boo behind the clouds seemed hopeless. What a lunatic she had been!

She picked up the pages and looked at his response. Such tenderness. Anticipation. Exhilaration. Trust. Confidence. Even fondness. The fact that Frank had ended his e-mail on a new level of familiarity had not escaped her attention.

She got up from the table and began to pace the floor. For the first time he had mentioned Sally. Actually, bared his feelings about her. Dared to be vulnerable. Just what she always wanted in a man. It showed great self-esteem and a capability of soul-to-soul encounter.

She looked at the ceiling in anguish. *He* was ready for a relationship, but was *she*? No! *No!* Not with her limp! Yet, if she didn't go through with the meeting, she would be rejecting his vulnerability, plunging a dagger into the chest of feelings he had bared to her. Crushing his trust in women. Perhaps sentencing him to a life of loneliness.

She sat at the table and fingered the pages. She couldn't accuse him of having paranoid tendencies. Look at how he trusted her! He gave her all this information for a book in the absence of any sort of agreement. Of course, she would never violate that trust, but how could *he* know?

She hoped she had not inadvertently misled him about her childhood. Naturally, it had obviously been a little unusual, a single mother raising twelve children and all that. It could be termed as trying at times. But not difficult! And certainly not unhappy. Her spirit leapt for joy when she remembered those carefree days. It was her life *now* that was difficult! Indeed, her spirit had crawled into a corner, afraid to make one move without Ken's approval.

She paced the floor again. She should not have been so definite with Frank. She should have said she would *try* to meet him in Pittsburgh during that week, not that she *would* do so! How could she have been so stupid?

There was no way she could meet him. Her limp was simply too humiliating for her. Why did they have to meet anyway? After all, this was the modern age of technology. Paths crossed because of increased technology. Frank himself said that. So, agreements could also be signed with the help of technology. Maybe Frank would go along with this.

Whom was she kidding? Of course he wouldn't. How could anyone collaborate on a book with a person he had never met? Too much mistrust would exist—even in their case, as cousins. One needed to see the proposed partner's face, watch the nonverbal language of the other person in order to reach agreements. This wasn't possible through e-mail yet. She put a pot on the stove for tea.

Besides, Frank had expressed interest in meeting her, in hearing her voice, in "testing his imagination against reality." She wondered what he was imagining. He had never seen her, not even a photograph of her. He knew her age, though. That was clear from the descendants' chart.

Maybe she should give him a call from Carol's. Maybe he would be satisfied if he heard her voice.

And she could send him a picture! A picture wouldn't reveal her limp. Maybe that would be enough *reality* for him.

Katie put a tea bag into the cup, poured hot water over it, and then sat at the table while it steeped. What if it *was* fate that had brought them together? Too many unique circumstances had taken place for it to have been sheer chance. But if they were predestined to meet, what happened if they didn't act on it? Was fate unacted upon harmful? On the other hand, fate was fate. By definition there was no way to *act on it*. If Frank and she did *not* meet, it was bunk to say they had been predestined to meet—but chose not to.

She realized she was at crossroads with Frank. What if she blew it by not meeting him? What if, in exasperation, he threw the whole idea away? What harm might she inflict on herself by blaming *fate* for the consequences of her own cowardice? What harm might she inflict on Frank? Was that what the expression "tempting fate" meant?

Katie got up and checked on her tea. She pressed the bag against the side of the cup with a spoon, discarded it, then fanned the tea to cool it a little. She decided it was too hot to sip yet, so returned to the table without it. In anquish, she pounded the table with her fists. Was there no way out of her predicament?

Fate or no fate, she was certain *she* would suffer if Frank bowed out of her life. She depended on his words for strength, for staying on an even keel. How many times a day did she retrieve his letters from their hiding place? Hold them to her bosom? Breathe in deeply? Feel his strength enter her body?

"Oh my God!" she exclaimed, suddenly remembering that another partner would have to be informed of this collaboration endeavor. She would *have* to tell Ken! He would be *furious*!

The floor groaned as she paced it once more. How had

she gotten herself into such a bind? She should have been honest with Ken from the beginning. Perhaps the lion she'd surely have to face might have snarled rather than charged with a deafening roar. But even a snarl would have forced her to put Frank out of her life.

Katie felt like a cornered deer. There was no way out. She returned to the table, picked up Frank's letter, and held it to her breast. Tears came to her eyes and her hands shook as she remembered her wedding day.

*** 

"Rain all day for the 25th," the weatherman said. Yet that morning Katie awoke to beautiful blue skies. She looked out her bedroom window and could not see a cloud on the horizon in any direction. She took it as a good omen for her marriage.

She threw open the window and inhaled the crisp morning air. The huge maple just outside her window was now fully leafed. A bluebird landed on a limb and, as if prompted by her 'appearance, began to sing.

"Oh, how kind of you to wish me happiness upon my wedding day," said Katie. "I'm going to miss you. Good-bye. And say good-bye to your lovely wife and peeps as well. I wish I could say I'll see you tomorrow, the next day, the next week, but I'll be far away. I'm leaving for Arkansas tomorrow."

The bluebird continued his lovely song.

"So, Mr. Bluebird, although this will be the happiest day of my life because I am marrying a man I love deeply, it will also be sorrowful since I must say good-bye to my family and friends, all of whom I also love deeply."

The bluebird sang more sweetly.

"I see my lament doesn't trouble you. It shouldn't. You *should* be happy, always singing a song of joy. For indeed, you are the luckiest of all creatures in the animal kingdom."

"Tweet, tweet."

"You wonder why? It's because you have wings. You can fly away whenever you want. You're so free! You don't know how lucky you are.

"I wouldn't worry at all about today if I had wings. I'd marry Ken, go with him to Arkansas, cuddle in his nest. Then, whenever I wanted to, I'd use my wings to fly away.

"I wouldn't fly away to just anywhere. I'd come back here. Frequently. Maybe every day for awhile. Come back to the warmth of my mother, my brothers and sisters, my friends.

"And someday I'll have little peeps of my own. Hopefully, very soon. As soon as they hatch, I'll teach them to fly. We'll fly together, then sit on your branch and sing happy songs with you."

The bluebird hopped around on the branch, then flicked his tail up and down.

"You're asking me about Ken? Will he be flying with me? I don't know. Unfortunately, Ken doesn't have a good relationship with his parents. They won't even be attending our wedding. He says it's because they had prior vacation plans, but his sister Karen told me a different story.

"She said Ken *told* his parents not to come to his wedding. Something about a 'falling-out' they had a few years ago, and he didn't want them to ruin his happy day. I can't understand all this.

"So now you know my fear, and what dampens my happiness on my wedding day. Even though Ken grew up in Pittsburgh, I'm afraid he will not wish to return for visits, at least not as often as I wish. I'll have to come alone, just me and my lovely peeps, that is."

"One last adjustment on your veil," said Katie's mother, in a dressing room at the LeMont. "Your French twist is causing the problem."

"How about my dress? Does it look all right?"

"It looks fine. I'm glad you decided on this off-the-shoulder satin. It plunges a little. A hint, but reveals nothing. It's flattering, yet simple. I'm glad we put the beading on the capped sleeves. And the skirt. It's not too long, is it?"

Katie winked at her mother. "Lucky for me you sew. Otherwise, I'd be in a street dress. You can't have a wedding dress as lovely as this in a couple of weeks, unless you have a lot of pull with someone who sews. Thanks for your help."

"Not just my help. Your sisters helped also."

"I'm very lucky to have such a loving and supportive family. We've always worked together and helped each other. It's like we're one big unit. Not all families are that way."

"I know you're thinking about Ken. It hurts you that Ken's mother and father won't be here for the wedding, doesn't it? But they have a logical reason. They couldn't cancel European vacation plans at the last minute."

Katie decided not to reveal what Karen had confided to her.

As she slipped into her white satin shoes, Katie said only, "I'm grateful his brother Bruce is best man, and to have Karen here as well."

"Be sure and introduce them to me. And maybe sometime when you and Ken come back for a visit, we'll have his mother and father over to the house for dinner."

Katie walked around the room in her satin heels and tested the soles for slipperiness. "That sounds like a good idea, Mother. How's Rebecca doing? Is she about ready?"

"I'll check. Oh, here she comes now."

Rebecca's street-length yellow dress had a large bow at the waist in the back. She wore a matching ribbon in her hair. "How do I look?" She laughed: "I feel so fancy in this."

"You look gorgeous," Katie laughed with her. "Just think! When we were little girls playing together in the sandbox, we never imagined we'd have dresses like these."

An usher arrived to escort Katie's mother to her seat. Then

the organist began to play a processional. "That's your cue, Rebecca. Here's your flowers."

Rebecca entered the room and stood in front of the altar positioned in front of a glass expanse overlooking the union of the three great rivers. Bruce and Ken were already there.

The music stopped while a white satin runner was unrolled to the altar. Katie peeked into the banquet room, which the restaurant staff had decorated and beautifully metamorphosed into a wedding chapel. The satin runner ended where Ken stood waiting for her.

The organist began playing Felix Mendelssohn's "Wedding March" from *A Midsummer Night's Dream*. Keeping her eyes on Ken, Katie carefully matched satin shoe to satin runner as she made her way to his side.

"How handsome he looks," she thought, "his tuxedo, his shirt and tie all in white. And Bruce looks nice, too. But I'm particularly happy to have Rebecca at my side today to calm my nerves."

Soon the wedding ceremony was over. Katie and Ken stood at the head of the receiving line and graciously accepted congratulations from family and friends. Katie looked at her left hand, then at Ken's. They had exchanged rings, so they must have repeated wedding vows. But she couldn't remember any of it. She wondered if she had been caught up in love's intoxicating power. Or perhaps it was the exquisite room and the view of the three rivers that had diverted her attention. Or maybe the blend of fragrances from her cascade of gardenias and lilies had muddled her memory.

While Katie and Ken posed for photographs, their guests enjoyed drinks, hors d'oeuvres and canapés in an adjoining dining room. Everyone savored the wonderful views of Pittsburgh as they conversed happily with each other. The blissful couple soon joined them for champagne toasts and chatted until dinner was announced.

After dining and cutting the wedding cake, Katie and Ken

bid good-bye to some of the guests who wished to leave. Most stayed on for dancing.

A pianist, a guitarist and a violinist tuned up in a corner. Soon the melodious chords of "The Hawaiian Wedding Song" waltzed through the air. "May I have this dance with my lovely wife?" asked Ken.

"You certainly may, and may this be the first of many beautiful days of dancing with you."

Ken and Katie held each other very closely as they whirled around the floor. Then they parted to dance with others. Everyone laughed and had a good time.

Katie was dancing with Bruce when Joe cut in. "My turn for a dance, Katie," he said.

"Oh, I'm glad you cut in," said Katie. "I have someone I want you to meet. Her name is Jenny."

"Okay, but first, let's just have this dance together." As they glided across the floor, Joe said, "I'm going to miss you so much, but when you get settled in Arkansas, I promise I'll visit you. I will be welcome, won't I?"

"Of course, Joe, always."

"I know I'll always be welcomed by *you*, but I mean, will Ken mind?"

"Will Ken mind? He'll be just as anxious for you to visit as I will. We're married now. A team. One unit. You've been such a good friend to me. I love you like a brother." Then she hugged him closely as they finished the dance.

"Come on, now. I want you to meet Jenny." Katie grasped Joe's hand and led him to the champagne table where Jenny was getting her glass filled.

"This is the Jenny that you've been talking about, the one you worked at Klein's with?"

"Yes, I've been wanting you to meet her for some time now. I think you two would be perfect together."

Suddenly Bruce was at Katie's side. "I hate to interrupt, Katie, but Ken is quite angry. He threw his carnation onto the floor, tried to grind it in with his shoe. I don't know why he's so ticked off."

Katie looked around. "Where is he?"

"He's gone. Stomped out of the room. I followed to see what he might do next."

Katie grabbed Bruce's arm. "What did he do? Where is he?"

"He had an argument with the limo driver, then grabbed the keys. He drove off, wheels screaming and screeching. I tell you Katie. He's really mad!"

Katie led Bruce toward the door. "Why would he be mad? What possibly could have upset him?"

"I don't know. It happened while you were dancing with Joe. He has a temper at times. Always has had."

"Oh, surely that wouldn't have upset him. He knows Joe is like a brother to me."

"I don't know, Katie. All I can tell you is what I saw."

Bruce and Katie exited the door. She looked around. The limo was nowhere in sight. "Where do you think he went?"

"Probably to your hotel room. I mean, your clothing, your luggage, everything is there. If it were me, that's where I'd go anyway."

"Our hotel. Oh, sure. I'll go right away."

"He took the limo. Remember?"

"Well, then I'll get a cab."

"Just wait here. I'll get one for you."

Katie tried her best to ignore the questioning glances of the taxi driver. Soon she arrived at the William Penn. Fortunately for her, Bruce had paid the cab fare plus tip before she left the restaurant, for she had no money.

She climbed the few steps and walked into a magnificent lobby, the elegant Palm Court. Soft music entered her ears, but she held her head high, refusing to look to the right or left. She dared not catch the eyes of curious onlookers at the restaurant, for fear she'd dissolve like a microwaved ice cube into nothing more than a puddle on the floor. Finally, she saw the elevators and sighed in relief.

She mentally reviewed the brochure Ken had shown her: The Renaissance Suite. The eighth floor.

The eighth floor! She worried about what she might find. And why was Ken angry?

The elevator lifted as smoothly as a hot air balloon and deposited Katie into a magnificent hall. Pleasure replaced thoughts of concern as she feasted on the splendor: the crown molding, the chair railings, paneling, too inviting not to caress! She ran her hands along all she could touch.

She remembered reading in the brochure that Jackie Gleason had stayed there. And so had Lawrence Welk, Liberace, President Eisenhower and presidential candidate John F. Kennedy. Had they rubbed their hands along the paneling as she, or were more pressing thoughts upon their minds?

Dazzling crystal chandeliers decorated the ceilings, like jewels in a night sky. She felt like she was in the country again. Lying on carpeted grass. Enraptured by twinkling constellations. Then she saw the French doors at the end of the hall and her distress returned.

Ken's words came back to her. "Go through the first set of doors. You'll see the bedroom at your left. But if you continue and go through the second set, a marvelous dining area awaits you." He then described adjoining sitting rooms on each side of the dining area, and some other rooms as well. Now, however, Katie was interested only in the bedroom. She wanted to freshen up. To think about what could possibly have angered Ken.

The glistening brass doorknob seemed to say, "Come pluck me," as if it was the apple in the Garden of Eden. Katie reached for the knob, then withdrew. Why couldn't she just stay in this delightful hall tonight? Sleep on its plush carpeting? Let the crystal constellations sing tinkling lullabies to her on her wedding night?

But a bride lying on the floor outside her honeymoon door would undoubtedly cause raised eyebrows, if not alarm. And shouldn't she find out what possibly could have angered Ken? She wondered where he was in the suite. In the dining room? The sitting room?

A flicker of hope flashed through her brain. Maybe he wasn't angry! Maybe he was sick. After all, Bruce had not talked with him, just observed him from a distance. Surely that must be it.

She tried the French door. She was grateful it was unlocked, for she had no key. The bedroom door was to her left.

First, she should search for Ken, help him with his problem. But she needed a few minutes alone, so she quietly pushed open the bedroom door.

When she did, a shocking scene slammed her. There sat the man she had just married like a tiger ready to pounce upon its prey. His face was hideously flushed and swollen. His blazing hot eyes locked onto hers, huge "Valerie" pupils just daring her to enter the room.

She couldn't stand them and looked at the floor. Bruce was right. This was the look of a very angry man.

The electrified room raised the hairs on her arms. She wished she had never opened that door. Why hadn't she spent the night in the hall? Now it was too late!

She froze, unsure of what to do next, then shot a quick glance at Ken. His eyes were on her. Wide open eyes! He was not going to give her even a half second to dart out of the room!

She looked around to consider her options. There was her suitcase next to the bathroom door. Maybe she could snatch that, flee into the bathroom. Pretend that she was sick. Hold her stomach as she ran. Certainly Ken wouldn't want her throwing up in front of him! On him!

Ah, she made it. She locked the door. She closed her eyes and felt the room sway. Gradually, a calmness washed over her. She was safe here. She could breathe. And think! She needed to think.

She took off her wedding gown, hung it over the shower bar, then splashed cold water on her face, her arms. There, that felt better. Now she could think.

She wondered what was really going on? According to Bruce, it had happened while she danced with Joe. Was she not allowed to dance with others? Ken had danced with other girls. It couldn't be that.

What could have caused his anger? She couldn't imagine. She must ask him. Perhaps something else . . . Or maybe someone else? Surely that was it. Someone had set him off. Why did she think she was to blame?

She felt better now and put on her pink, satin negligee, smoothing the gown against her skin. The deep cut stopped just short of her nipples. She unpinned her long blond hair and let it flow over her shoulders. A little dab of Chanel No. 5 on her wrist. His favorite. She felt strengthened and ready to try again.

She listened at the door. It was quiet in the bedroom. Maybe too quiet. Was he still in his tuxedo? Glaring? Daring? Maybe he had fallen asleep. Oh, did she hope so!

She unlocked the door, slowly, silently, then opened it just a crack. He saw it. His eyes flashed a signal that told her retreat was out of the question. She had to enter the room.

She would not crawl into that room! She would stroll. For what had she done after all? He was not going to make her crawl!

But she could retreat. Quickly run into the bathroom. Lock the toilet stall. No! She was no longer an Old Order Mennonite. She did not have to turn the other cheek, behave like a meek lamb in front of a lion.

She walked into the room with her head held high. His lips formed an ugly curl. The fire that shot from his eyes hit her like a stun gun. She dropped into a chair.

"You whore!" he yelled. "You asshole!" And such awful words that spewed from his lips came at her like knives, stabbing over and over again.

Ken came over and straddled her. His legs pinned her in the chair. His sickening hot breaths slapped against her skin. She turned her face aside.

"Do you really think you can come in here and pretend you did nothing wrong? You bitch! I saw you dance with Joe. Cheek to cheek! Thigh to thigh! You treat me like this on our wedding day! You're one hell of a bitch!"

Katie tried to protest, to scream it wasn't so! But her head may as well have been filled with swarming insects. All she could manage was a weak gasp.

Ken got off of her and threw his tuxedo coat to the floor. He undid his tie and threw it across the room. Katie covered her eyes. She could watch no more.

"Oh, so you don't want to see me! Good! Because I'm leaving anyway! I've got to get out of here! You piss me off so much, I don't know what I might do next!" He slammed the door as he left.

Katie didn't remember it, but she must have gone to bed at some point. For she awoke from time to time. Sometimes she sobbed so hard the bed shook. At other times, she beat the pillows into pulp. All this intermingled with fitful dreams.

By early morning she was furious. How could this have happened? What had she done wrong? Nothing! To think he was mad at her simply for dancing with Joe! He knew Joe was just a good friend from high school. She had never even dated him. She should have a right to male friends.

She would not be treated this way. She'd fight back! She'd get up, get dressed, and get out of there. When he came back, she'd be gone. Ha! He could find someone else to move with him to Arkansas. She wasn't crazy about going there anyway. She'd rather stay in Pittsburgh with her family than go there with a—a bad-tailed rooster. Yes, that was exactly what he was—a bad-tailed rooster!

That thought brought a slight smile to her face, which was further enhanced by the first rays of the morning sun cheerfully peeking around the edges of the heavy drapes. It looked so warm, so nourishing that she parted the drapes to drink in its early morning loveliness.

Like a newcomer to Florentine opera, Katie was treated unexpectedly to a magnificent scene. There, spotlighted by the sun, stood an awesome architectural achievement: the gothic edifice of the Union Trust Bank. Katie could scarcely contain her emotions. As a person used to experiencing the world through touching, she wanted to fly and run her hands across the spires, the pillars, the dormers, the structure. Covering it all, like frosting decorating a cake, were the many sculptured masonry details in designs of swirls, flourishes, and drapes. The beauty bewitched her.

But soon it ended with the sound of a key entering a lock—a door opening.

There stood Ken, dressed just as he had been when he left last night. The sight of him made her recoil, although she was relieved to see that his flushed and swollen face was gone. In fact, what had been fire in his eyes now was passion.

He smiled and said, "Good morning, Kitten!" as if nothing had happened.

He approached her, encircled her with his arms. She pulled back.

He tried again, this time drawing her in so closely that she thought she could feel his heart beating.

"How pretty you look in your negligee, Kitten!" He danced her around the room while kissing her lips, her neck. He moved slowly, kissing, caressing, loosening her gown. He danced her to the bed and gently eased her onto it.

He pulled her negligee down. She resisted every move. But finally he freed it, and tossed it onto the floor. He got on top of her, then smoothed her hair and kissed her again, but she lay there unresponsive, like a corpse in the morgue.

He ran his fingers over her brow and cheeks, drew designs on her face, then said, "Remember how you've always wanted a ranch on a hill and I've always wanted a colonial? I was thinking about it last night. I think I would like the ranch on the hill too."

Katie's ears perked up. Had she heard correctly? He was going to let her have the house she wanted?

She began to warm. He's sorry about last night. That's why he's agreeing to the ranch.

And maybe he was right. Maybe it *was* wrong of me to have danced so closely with Joe. A girl raised as an Old Order Mennonite simply did not know all the rules of the outside world. She had much to learn.

Katie no longer resisted, and a few moments later he entered her. Although she was no longer a corpse, neither was she very much alive. Her head could explain away his wedding night behavior but her body cells remembered and refused to empty their contents. If Ken noticed a bad taste in the soup that morning, it was because she hadn't added any ingredients of her own.

***

A ringing telephone snapped Katie out of her wedding thoughts. She ran to answer it.

"Hi, Kitten. What are you doing?"

"Oh, I'm just finishing up the breakfast dishes."

"At this late hour? It's nearly noon."

"I started straightening out my cupboards this morning and time got away from me."

"Well, what I called to tell you is the seminar has been called off. The main speaker had a heart attack. He's okay, but will need a couple months to recuperate."

"Oh, I'm sorry to hear that," Katie said. But she wasn't. Her problem was solved! She was grateful a leaping heart could not be detected over the telephone.

"Well, those things happen. But what it means is I'll be home after all. Could you call your mother and tell her your plans have changed and that you'll visit her later on this summer? Maybe in a month. I have a business engagement in California then. Thanks, Kitten. Got to get back to work. See you around five. Love you. Bye."

Katie couldn't believe her good fortune. She now had an excuse for Frank! She wouldn't be able to meet him on the sixteenth because of Ken's change in plans.

Now, with the foolish ideas of running through pastures out of her head at last, she would suggest handling the agreement by e-mail. She wrote her letter.

> *Dear Frank,*
>
> *It is with deep regret that I must tell you I'll be unable to meet with you in Pittsburgh on the sixteenth. My husband's seminar plans have been canceled because the main speaker had a heart attack. So now I am unable to go to visit my family that week. Perhaps we can meet at some later date.*
>
> *I enjoyed the story about Johann's emigration to the U.S. immensely. I am impressed with your ability to fictionalize genealogy, and have no doubt you and I could work well together on a book.*
>
> *Which brings me to a subject I'd like to raise with you. Since we cannot meet shortly as we planned, I am wondering if you would draw up an agreement regarding our book collaboration. E-mail it to me. I'll look it over, make any comments or changes I think might be appropriate, then e-mail it back to you. Naturally, we will also need signed hard copies. We can handle that by "snail mail," as they say.*
>
> *Thanks for sharing the story of Sally with me. It must*

*have been terrible for you to lose her like that. It warms my heart to know that some of my earlier comments brought you solace and strength.*

*I must tell you your letters have brought untold strength and happiness to me. You mentioned feeling that a difficult childhood such as mine produced creative minds. I do not think of my childhood as difficult, but rather, loving, happy and joyous. Unfortunately, I would not use those adjectives to describe my adulthood.*

*This letter will be short as I wanted to inform you as early as possible about the cancellation of our proposed meeting date. If it is agreeable to you, please draft up an agreement and e-mail it to me.*

She wondered how to end the letter. After all, "fondly" meant affectionately. She felt much affection for him. Should she end with that?

"There you go with your fantasies again," Katie scolded herself. She typed, "Fondly, Katie," saved the letter to a diskette, and later e-mailed it from Carol's.

# 9

## THE MELTED FACE

After sending Frank the e-mail, Katie wanted to crawl into a dumpster. She decided to go to bed early and told Ken she had a headache. But it was a heartache. She tossed and turned for what seemed like hours before finally falling asleep.

She awoke to her own scream. She dragged legs that felt like lead into the bathroom and turned on the light. Hesitantly, she looked into the mirror. She breathed a sigh of relief. It wasn't true. Yet it had all seemed so real, it left her feeling like someone had picked her up and slammed her against a wall.

It made no sense returning to bed and trying to go back to sleep. Not with such a dream knocking around at her body walls. Such a dream would never leave without interpretation.

She grasped the handrails as she descended the stairs, then shakily made her way into the great room. She looked out the window. The golf course was pitch black. The hall clock struck four. The sound of it sent nerves discharging throughout her body, like popcorn kernels exploding when heated in hot oil. She needed to calm down. This was no time for coffee. She needed chamomile tea.

With cup in hand, she sipped the tea and paced the floor. She went over the dream again and again in her mind. What could it have meant? She was on her fourth cup of tea when the cheerful eyes of the sun peeked over the horizon. But Katie never saw it. For her, it was night. She knew the dream was somehow connected with that awful e-mail she had sent Frank.

Like a dog accustomed to hearing its master's every move, she heard Ken's bathroom tinkle, the downpour of his shower. the buzz of his shaver, the whirl of his electric toothbrush. Then followed some gargling, hacking, and several loud coughs to clear his throat. She heard the shuffle of hangers in the closet, the opening and closing of drawers. These familiar sounds had become an irritant to her, like pollen to an allergy sufferer. Yet, when he appeared fully dressed and groomed in the kitchen, neither he nor anyone else would have guessed she had these feelings, so skillfully had she mastered the art of camouflaging nonverbal messages.

Dutifully, she went about her usual morning routine. She squeezed three oranges for his juice, fixed him a cup of coffee, poured his cereal into a bowl, sliced a banana onto it, added milk and a spoon. She placed the newspaper in front of him.

She hoped he wouldn't ask any questions, like about the dream she had last night. He knew about it, of course, because her scream had awakened him. Strangely, though, he didn't inquire about the dream, but only about her headache of the previous evening.

She wished he hadn't said anything because her heartache was beyond concealment. It shot such painful spasms onto her face, that she had to turn her back to him and rinse dishes in the sink. Why didn't he leave for work!

Finally, she helped him into his jacket and gave him an obedient *hurry-and-get-out-of-here* kiss for the day.

She wondered if it was too early to call Carol, who, she knew, liked to sleep in during the summer months. She looked at the clock. It was seven-thirty.

She waited until eight before succumbing. She dialed Carol's number.

"We're a little early, aren't we?"

"Oh, I'm sorry, Carol. I just couldn't stand it another moment. I have to talk with you."

"Well, go on. I'm up now."

"No, I don't mean over the telephone. I had a terrible dream last night. I'm sure it was prompted by that e-mail I sent to Frank. Can you get an e-mail back once you send it?"

"No, I don't think so. But Katie, are you so sure you said something you wouldn't want him to read? I've never known you to do something like that."

"Oh, I did. I am so sorry about it now."

"Tell you what," Carol said. "Let me get dressed. I'll come over and, while I bum some morning coffee off you, you can tell me about your dream."

"Oh, thanks, Carol. This dream is like an electric mixer inside me, with beaters going at top speed. I'm so upset. I know it has a deep meaning."

Fifteen minutes later Carol was at her door. Katie had a pot of coffee awaiting her. She filled two cups. They sat at the kitchen table and took their first sips.

"Well, Katie. What has you so disturbed?"

"I have really stooped to a new low. You know how Frank has been wanting to meet me. We set it up for when I was to be in Pittsburgh. For the sixteenth. But of course—don't roll your eyes over this—I didn't want him to see my limp.

"Yesterday Ken told me the seminar was called off, so I had an excuse for not meeting Frank. I was actually happy! That's how despicable I have become."

"You and your limp," Carol said disparagingly. "Boy, are you going to lead an unhappy life unless you get over that!"

"In that e-mail I sent, I told him I couldn't meet him. Though at one level I was glad for the excuse, down deep I felt crummy. Frank has been so nice and considerate to me, and look how I treat him! So last night, when I had that terrible dream, I just know it's all connected."

"Pretty strong coffee," said Carol as she added cream and sugar to it. "Okay, so you have a couple of things disturbing you and you think they're interconnected. Now tell me your dream."

"I have to warn you, it's long. It's one of those dreams that etch every detail onto the brain."

"So? I'm having my morning coffee. Start talking."

"I was sitting right there, on the floor of that room." Katie pointed to the great room. "I had just polished my nails, so I was sitting on the carpet and shaking my hands to get the polish to dry.

"Just then Ken strutted into the room. He was fully dressed in his best black Avanti suit. You know the one. He really looks nice in it.

"'Aren't you ready yet?' he asked me. I didn't like the tone of his voice.

"I admitted I wasn't, but I was a little bothered by his asking me because I thought I still had plenty of time.

"'Well, you better not make me late!' he growled. 'You know how important this evening is to me.'

"Though I was sure it was *not* getting late, I didn't want a confrontation, so immediately got up from the floor and started toward the bathroom. I assured him that I wouldn't be long since my dress was pressed and my hair already done.

"I was certain Ken had originally told me to be ready at six, and it was now only five, so I had this uneasy feeling as I hurried to the bathroom. Why was he rushing me? I wondered. I didn't want to ask *him*, though, because I was afraid he might get mad. I didn't want the evening spoiled. For it was no small evening we were having. We were invited to a banquet at the residence of the governor and first lady.

"As soon as I entered the bathroom, I turned on the shower and scrubbed my body with that freesia gel, the one I love so much. As usual, my mind went into a fragrance high. Bubbles in my bath; bubbles in my head. My nose seems to be my instrument for putting a little heaven on my earth.

"But my conscious brain rudely interrupted my olfactory one when I thought of Ken waiting impatiently for me. I quickly rinsed and dried myself. All I had to do now was apply a little makeup and get dressed.

"Until that point, I had not looked into the bathroom mirror. And this is where the awful part begins."

Katie freshened their cups of coffee before continuing the story.

"I looked into the mirror and saw a face I didn't recognize. It was horrible. But naturally, I knew it was me. Who else was in the bathroom?

"My heart pounded so hard, I could feel each thump in my head. The pounding, or the face in the mirror, swarmed my brain and I had to hold onto the sink to steady myself. Then nausea overcame me, and I thought I was going to throw up. Carol, all of this seemed so real that I am unable to know even now if any of it actually took place.

"Anyway, I lowered my head, which undoubtedly caused blood to return to my brain. I began to think about that awful face. I thought maybe I had imagined it and decided to take a peek. I covered my eyes with my hands, then spread my fingers just enough to allow the tiniest glimpse. A horrible face, eyes covered with spread fingers, peeked back at me.

"But Carol. Now comes the really weird part. As upset as I was about my face, I remembered that Ken was waiting for me. I didn't want to make him mad.

"I braced myself, then took a full look in the mirror. My facial structures, skin and eyes looked like molten wax flowing down the side of a candle. It was horrible.

"But horrible as it was, I worried about Ken's reaction to it. I knew he'd be enraged about this. I'd spoil his evening for sure.

"However, I worried more about making him late, so put on makeup as best I could and slipped into that black dress from Dillard's. Remember it? You were with me when I bought it.

"Well, the dress went on nicely. I added a string of pearls, then pearl drops at my ears. Some black hosiery and heels, and I was ready to leave the bathroom. Notice I'm not mentioning a limp. The only good part of this dream was I didn't have my limp.

"I joined Ken who was sitting at the bar sipping an old-fashioned. 'Here,' he says, 'I made one for you,' and he hands me a glass. 'You look very pretty tonight. Is that a new dress? I don't think I've seen it before.'

"You can imagine how shocked I was that he hadn't mentioned my melted face. So I just tried to keep a cool outside demeanor while inside I was churning. Why is he talking about my dress and not recoiling in horror over my face? I wondered. That would have been his typical reaction. But he said nothing about my face.

"We finished our drinks, put the glasses in the kitchen, and locked up the house. Then we got into our Town Car and soon were driving down highway 89 toward I-40. The old-fashioned must have made me forget my predicament, for now I remember that Ken and I were soon conversing and laughing as we drove toward Little Rock."

Katie paused to scowl at the gagging sounds Carol made over the word *laughing*.

Then she continued. "We were about half way to the governor's residence when the vision of my melted face shot back into my mind. It puzzled me greatly that Ken hadn't mentioned it, because you know Ken. No pretending with him. He tells things like they are. This made me think maybe he really couldn't see it. After all, he would never take me to meet the governor and first lady with a melted face.

"I toyed with the idea that perhaps it was our bathroom

mirror rather than my face that was distorted. Maybe my face was fine. I convinced myself that this was what it was. A defective mirror. That's all. I began to feel better.

"Buoyed with this new belief, I decided to test my theory. I flipped down the sun visor, turned on the light, and looked into that mirror. The anguished sigh that escaped my lips made Ken look over at me.

"'What's the matter with you?' he asked. 'Don't you like the way you look? I think you look very pretty tonight.'

"At this point I was even more confused. On one hand, I knew for sure that Ken could not see my melted face. On the other hand, I could no longer delude myself into thinking it stemmed from a distorted mirror. So I entertained other ideas as to how my face could possibly be that way. I decided that maybe I was the *only* one who could see it.

"Before long, our Town Car pulled up to the open gate at the governor's residence. The guard matched our identification to the guest list, then invited us to enter. The driveway circled to a stop in front of the mansion. A white-gloved valet approached the car.

"The pace of my heart set a new world record as doubts returned to me. I wondered if it was true that no one other than myself could see my melted face. Maybe it was just hidden from Ken. Who knew for what reason?

"I realized at this point I had a perfect opportunity to find out for sure by exposing my face to the valet. If I horrified him, then I knew others would be able to see my melted face too. Far better to test it on this one solitary individual rather than on the masses of distinguished banquet guests I would soon meet, don't you think so?"

Carol said nothing and took a sip of coffee.

"But I didn't have the nerve to do it! Coward that I was, I hid my face from him and awaited the verdict of hundreds of the social elite.

"The reception line was already long and we filed in at

the end. Greetings of 'How are you,' 'So nice to see you,' and 'You look so good tonight,' filled the air. I tried my best to meet each pleasantry with an in-kind message, but my face was hot from the rapid pace of electrical firings within my brain. And these firings weren't speaking kindly to me. One of them said, 'Don't you know this is a social affair!' Another said, 'These people will never mention your melted face even if they see it! They've been trained since childhood not to reveal their inner thoughts.'

"But I could see my reflection in the pupils of their widely opened eyes, and I saw my melted face. I let out a sharp scream and collapsed onto the mansion grounds.

"The next thing I knew Ken was yelling at me. 'What the hell's wrong with you!' Apparently my scream had scared him into a 'straight up' sitting position. He mumbled something about me interrupting his sleep in such a horrible manner, then grunted a few times before reclining again. Shortly, he resumed his snoring.

"But for me, the dream seemed so real that I had to go check the bathroom mirror. When I did, I was most relieved to learn it was all a dream! I didn't sleep another wink all night.

"It's with me, Carol. It's in me, and I can't get it out!"

"You don't do anything in moderation, do you Katie? Even your dreams are dramatic! Now, why do you think this one relates to Frank?"

"Because, don't you see? I used Ken as my excuse for not meeting Frank. It was a despicable, ugly thing to do. That's why I had such a despicable, ugly face in my dream."

"That might *not* be the reason for your dream at all, Katie. It might be that Ken is taking over your mind, a process symbolized by the melting face. Think about it! You saw your face as melting, because, down deep, you realized you were losing your mind. Not in the sense of going crazy mentally, but rather of having your personality totally subjugated by

Ken. Everyone else saw the same thing. Everyone *except Ken*, of course. *He* couldn't see your melting face, because, for him, you never had a mind to lose. You were just a doll with no independent existence.

"Now you tell me, what does that really have to do with you and Frank?"

"Oh, I never thought of it that way."

"Of course not, because, for all intents and purposes, Ken practically *has* taken over your mind. Heaven only knows, I'm not a dream interpreter or a counselor, but I am your best friend, so I can see a lot of things in your dream that you, lacking an independent mind, cannot.

"For instance, do you scream when you first see your melted face? No. You worry about whether Ken will be angry with you for being late. So you go ahead and get dressed, trying to pretend nothing is wrong.

"Do you throw a towel over head when you first approach Ken with your melted face? No. You present yourself naked, so to speak, because you're so worried about his anger.

"You go all the way across town and subject yourself to the ridicule of hundreds of the social elite, as you call them, rather than make Ken mad. His anger controls your mind and your behavior. You make decisions that allow you to step around Ken's rages. And I bet you're scared to death that Ken will learn you're corresponding with Frank by using my e-mail program."

"Oh, he'd be terribly mad about that."

"That's what the melted face is all about. Remember that you didn't have your limp in the dream. Of course not, because your limp has nothing to do with who you are. It's Ken that defines you, controls you, gives you the ugly, melted face."

"Don't say that!" Katie buried her face in her hands.

"Oh, I'm sorry, I'm sorry. I didn't mean to hurt you." Carol hugged Katie. "It's just that when the revelation came to me, it blew me away. You poor, dear girl, you're by no means alone. There are many women in your shoes."

"People like Jenny can open their blouses and show the world their wounds," Katie said softly. "But *some scars are within, like scarred hearts and scarred spirits.* These cannot be shown to others."

"Huh? Where did you hear that?"

"It's just something my dear sweet girlfriend in Pittsburgh said to me one time. It was before I got married."

"What I don't understand is how someone would allow herself to be taken over so completely as you have."

"Upbringing, I guess. Being taught that the man is to be obeyed *regardless*. Also, being taught to turn the other cheek. And you *know* how many girls are taught to be sweet above all else. I think these teachings stick with you throughout life."

"So, why don't you have the gumption to leave?"

"One word, Carol. Fear."

"Oh, very good, Katie! I was mistaken. Your mind doesn't belong totally to Ken. Not with that kind of thinking."

"It's become a 'Catch 22' situation," Katie said. "Fear of staying, obviously; but also fear of leaving. It's like being under Ken's huge hand. Remember our conversation at Pizza Hut. The one you called a sickening scene!"

"Oh, I remember," said Carol. "And it *is* sickening!"

"It's a two-edged sword. Personal criticisms and belittling destroy my self-confidence; criticisms and belittling of everyone else fill the outside world with scary unknowns. The seed is planted. He is telling me: 'You don't have what it takes to make it on your own in this frightening world. You need my protection.' It creates total dependence, and fear of leaving.

"This doesn't just happen to women. It happens to men and children as well. It happens to employees. When criticisms and belittling destroy an employee's self-confidence, that employee becomes dependent and fears his or her ability to get a new job."

"It kind of cripples you in life," Carol offered. "Gives you a limp! Oh, wow! This is good. You plant these images in my head, and boom! I say what I see!"

Katie smiled at her friend's words. "I never thought of it that way, but you are right. Of course, that's not the reason for my limp. Mine is physical. A broken bone from an accident. But I do like the analogy."

"By the way Katie, you've never told me how the accident took place."

"I'm too exhausted to go into that today, Carol."

"Well, whenever. You can tell me anything, you know. But for now, I remember what you said at Pizza Hut, something about enlightenment and that you had turned your feet in a new direction. Wasn't it something like that?"

"I said that once my spirit realized what was going on, it demanded release, freedom. I am now clothed in the garments of enlightenment and they have given my feet a new direction."

Carol gave Katie a big hug. "And you're running, not walking anymore, right?"

"Right!"

"You're going to make it, kiddo! Come on. Let's get some breakfast."

"Thanks, Carol, but I think I should get some sleep, now that I feel so much better about my dream. I'm so lucky to have a good friend like you."

"So are you going to send Frank another e-mail?"

"Definitely! I'll tell him I'll meet him at the Reyher-Wilhelm barn. He wanted so much to see the farm. That'll be a good place for us to sign an agreement. But right now I've got to have a nap so I can think sensibly."

"What about Ken?"

"Oh, I forgot about him! Let me look at his calendar. I

see he has penned in an overnight trip next week. Thursday night, the seventeenth. He must have scheduled this after the seminar was canceled. One night. That's long enough for me to go to Columbiana, meet Frank, then return."

"Won't Ken call you?"

"He doesn't always on short trips. But if he does, I'll think of some excuse."

"Wow, that's great! Now get some sleep and I'll see you later."

Katie laid on the sofa and soon fell asleep. She dreamt this time about meeting Frank. She smiled a lot in her sleep.

# 10

## DUPED

About the same time Katie was enjoying her wonderful dreams about Frank, Bill popped his head into Frank's office. "Hi Frank," he said. "Ready for lunch?"

"You go ahead. I don't feel like lunch today. Actually, I don't feel like anything today."

"What's bummed you out? You've been in such a great mood ever since you started corresponding with that cousin of yours. Something go wrong?"

"Yeah. No. I don't know if I'd call it *wrong*. It's just that in her e-mail of last night . . . let's just say it wasn't something I wanted to hear."

"Come on. You've got to eat something. Tell me about it over lunch."

"Really, Bill, I'm in no mood to eat. It would leave a knot in my stomach. I'd pinned so much hope on meeting Katie in Pittsburgh shortly. Now it's off. Instead, she suggests I draft up an agreement on this book collaboration and *e-mail* it to her. I don't want that. I want to meet her. Sometimes I wonder if she's not saying something else between the lines."

"Like what?"

"Like, she doesn't *want* to meet me. Like, she has no intention of collaborating on a book with me."

"She's never left you with the impression that she didn't want to work on a book with you, has she?"

"No, she's not done that, but then again, I foolishly sent her everything I had. Now she comes back and says we can't meet."

"Oh, I can't believe you did *that*, Frank. You gave her *all* of it? Didn't hold anything back?"

Frank nodded disconsolately. "She seemed so interested. I had no reason to mistrust her. I guess in the end I got carried away in my attempts to impress her with my artistic abilities."

"I hate to be the one to put the word in your head, but it looks to me like you've been duped."

"Duped? No, I really don't think Katie would do that. I just can't figure out where she's coming from. She comes across as someone so sweet and kind in her letters. Someone with real substance. I've felt connected to her from the very beginning. She's in my head."

"How about your heart? It's a short distance from your head to your heart."

"For heaven's sake, Bill, she's married! And she's my cousin. Are you suggesting I have romantic feelings for her? It's just that we seem to think alike, and I know we could work very well together on a book."

"Sorry. I didn't mean to get under your skin."

"I thought we were all set to meet. She was going back to visit her family at a time when her husband would be out of town at some sort of seminar. She travels when he's out of town. Something about his not liking to be home alone. I don't know what that's about.

"It's such a short hop to Pittsburgh. I thought we could meet in a nice restaurant for lunch and talk about the book. It would have worked perfectly.

"Then last evening she wrote that her husband's seminar was canceled. The main speaker had a heart attack."

"They don't cancel seminars because the main speaker has a heart attack. They fill in with someone else."

"Well, I don't know about that."

"What new date did she give you?"

"She didn't. Like I said, she wants me to draft up the agreement, then e-mail it. I don't think I can do that. I feel compelled to put a face on the person I sign an agreement with."

"Can't you see, Frank? She doesn't need you anymore. You've given her your entire contribution. Now she can write the book by herself."

"Katie isn't like that!"

"Do you really know Katie?"

"Well I know she was raised as an Old Order Mennonite, and I know they are extremely honest people."

"But she's not Old Order now, is she?"

"Of course, not. Not with her using computers, e-mailing and all the other new technology."

"What does she look like?"

"I really don't know. We haven't discussed how we look or personal things like that. Why would we? All I know is that she has asked me to not mail anything to her—or telephone her. She didn't say why, but I get the impression it's related to her marriage, which apparently is not a happy one."

"Why do you think that?" Bill asked.

"Because of something she wrote in this last e-mail. She described her childhood as having been 'loving, happy and joyous' but said she wouldn't use those adjectives for her adulthood. I think probably her husband is a controlling and jealous person, and she's scared that he'll find out about our correspondence.

"She uses her girlfriend's Juno program for e-mailing. Yet I checked an e-mail address directory and found a Kenneth Krauss at America on Line. I suppose there could be another Kenneth Krauss among the two-hundred-fifty-million-plus Americans, but judging from my genealogical resource data, Krauss is not a common name, nor is Kenneth."

"So you think her husband doesn't know she's corresponding with you?"

"As far as I know, he doesn't."

"Does he know you exist?"

"I doubt it."

"Frank, it doesn't add up. Think about it. How are you ever going to collaborate on a book with Katie without her husband's knowing about you? She'll *never* agree to meet with you. A year from now, a bestseller will appear on the market. The author? None other than our little Ms. Katie Krauss."

Frank felt a hot mass creep down his face. He buried his face in his paperwork. "Really, Bill, she's not like that. Better get to the cafeteria and get your lunch while you still have time."

It ticked Frank off that Bill doubted Katie's sincerity. Nevertheless, the worm Bill inserted into his body began to wriggle, then multiply. Soon a host of worms squirmed and moved deeper as they easily passed from cell to cell. His body clamored for relief, but his mind resisted. Bill just didn't understand, he told himself. If he had read her letters, he'd have seen what she was truly like!

Katie was a sincere person. Interested in him. Interested in their common ancestry. Hadn't she inquired about them in every letter? Hadn't she encouraged him to divulge more and more of the story? Divulge more and more and more . . .

Flash! The worms entered Frank's brain. He suddenly saw a pattern of deception, of being led on, that he had earlier refused to believe. "Oh, shit," he said, softly but audibly. He rarely used four-letter words, and when he did, it was usually for good reason.

He went through the afternoon with his head in a fog. The doubt-worms ate at his stomach, crunched at his muscles, and had a banquet in his brain. Finally, he finished his day's work and was free to go home.

At each street corner, at each stoplight, at each long, winding road, the worms multiplied. He dragged his totally chewed-up body and mind into the house, then logged onto his computer. Only by composing a letter could he obtain the relief he required.

*Dear Katie,*

*What I have to say to you comes with much agony, but I feel I have no other choice.*

*In each of my e-mails to you, I expressed a desire to meet with you for the purpose of discussing our proposed COLLABORATIVE book project. I asked you to pick practically any location and time and said I would be there to meet you. You made excuses, excuses I did not understand. Your last excuse hurt me deeply, maybe because I had been overly excited about meeting you at last.*

*Perhaps, also, I feel wounded because I realize I have given you all of my information and story ideas regarding our common ancestry. Conceivably, you could now write a book without me and there's nothing I could do to stop you.*

*It numbs my mind to believe you would intentionally dupe me. Maybe I'm angry with myself for trusting in you, for sending you all the wonderful stories of our ancestors, for sharing with you the Pleidelsheim trip I took with my mother. I was a fool to have done all this.*

*How can we draft an agreement together through e-mail when I mistrust your motivations?*

*All I can say to you is that I am heartbroken to think you could treat me this way. You're the first person I felt connected with since my beloved wife died. Sally was my soul mate, and to tell you the truth, you were slipping into that slot as well.*

*But that's all over now. I feel betrayed. I guess it hurts so badly because I thought you were a different person. This is my farewell letter to you.*

*Frank.*

Frank sent the e-mail off immediately. The crunching of the worms subsided, but the ache in his heart made him bend over in pain.

# 11

## *AN ACT OF KINDNESS*

Katie still napped, unaware of the worm Bill had inserted into Frank's body. Her awful dream about her melted face left her so energy-depleted that she slept until two in the afternoon. Then she showered, put on fresh jeans and a t-shirt, tidied up the house a little and put a pork roast in the oven for dinner. She looked at the clock and was dismayed that so much time had passed. Disappointedly, she realized it was too late to write Frank now and suggest the new meeting date at the barn.

But if she delayed writing Frank until the morning, would this cause him some difficulty? She quickly decided it would not, since her proposed new time would be in the evening, and she was sure he worked days. After all, didn't he say he wrote fiction to fill up evening hours?

Oblivious to the worm problem Frank was having, she sang happy songs as she fixed potatoes and carrots to serve alongside the roast.

Later, after dinner, she stacked the dishes in the dishwasher and cleaned up the kitchen. She could see Ken in the great room nestled in his easy chair, half watching television, half sleeping.

She had one more task before she could join him: setting out the oranges for Ken's morning juice, which he liked at room temperature.

When she opened the refrigerator to take out the oranges, she realized she had only one left. She had intended to shop for more today, but, with the dream and all, she had forgotten. There wouldn't be enough to fill Ken's glass. She'd have to go to the store.

She peeked in to see if he was awake. His eyes were half open. She told him she had to run to the store for oranges.

"How long will you be gone?" he asked, sleepily.

"I'm just going to Templeton's. They're usually not busy at this time of night. Not more than a half-hour, at the most."

Katie grabbed her purse, got into her BMW, and headed for the store at about the same time Frank's disastrous letter hit Carol's in-box.

Unaware that anything was amiss, Katie motored down Mt. Carmel Road. The thick cloud cover caused an early dusk and she switched on her headlights. When she reached Highway 89, she waited for two cars to pass. The first, she noticed, was driven by an elderly lady; the second, by a man with a woman in the passenger seat holding a child. She turned right at the church.

No sooner had Katie made her turn when the elderly lady slowed down and signaled a right turn into a driveway. The second car had to brake almost to a complete stop. As it did, suddenly the passenger door opened and out jumped the woman with the child in her arms. They rolled as one unit into the ditch. With the passenger door still ajar, this second car accelerated and took off down the highway, leaving the woman and child behind.

Katie watched in total astonishment. She couldn't believe that the man would simply drive off, leaving his passengers in the ditch like that. She had to help!

She pulled off onto the shoulder, got out, and ran over to them, her car lights illuminating the way. She found the woman to be very young, about sixteen perhaps. Just a girl! "Are you hurt?" Katie asked.

"No Ma'am," the girl said, as she got to her feet and brushed herself and the little one off. She held the child closely, who, Katie could now see, was a little boy. Then she started to sob and the boy sobbed too.

Katie put a motherly arm around them, then said, "Come, sit in my car. You'll be more comfortable there. Then you can tell me what's wrong. What is your name anyway?"

"Maggie," said the girl between sniffs.

"Oh, what a pretty name, Maggie! And your little boy's?"

"Joh-n-n-y," Maggie said, as tears rolled down her cheeks.

"And Johnny, your name is pretty too," said Katie. She wished she had a tissue to offer Maggie.

"How old are you, Johnny?"

He looked at Katie, then buried his face in his mother's shoulder.

"Three," said Maggie, wiping her tears with her hands. "He's shy."

Katie helped them get into her car and then got behind the wheel again. She opened her purse and pulled out a couple of tissues for Maggie, who used them to wipe her eyes and blow her nose. Then Katie smiled and said, "Please, tell me what's wrong. I saw you jump out of that car—you with Johnny in your arms."

Maggie didn't respond. She just wiped her eyes and sniffled. Then Katie saw her shiver.

"Where were you going?"

Maggie finally looked up. "The store," she said. "I's goin for milk."

"Well, then, you're in luck, for that's just where I was going too. I'll take you there, and then home if you'd like."

Katie noticed the sniffles lessened.

"The store's just up the road. We'll be there in no time. Where do you live?"

"Lonoke," Maggie answered.

"Then you were headed in the wrong direction. Did you know that?"

"Yes, Ma'am."

"My name is Katie. Please call me Katie."

"Yes, Ma'am, ah, Ka-tie."

Katie praised her. "Oh, that sounds so much better." The girl's tears had stopped, and Johnny's big eyes were watching her.

"Do you like candy, Johnny?" she asked.

He didn't answer, but his smile revealed that the word had pleasant connotations for him.

"I'll get you a sucker at the store. Would you like that?"

A tentative grin appeared on Johnny's face as he glanced at his mother.

Maggie blew her nose and then sighed. For Katie, that was a sign she was getting somewhere.

Katie reflected. If Maggie were really only about sixteen, she would have been thirteen when Johnny was born. It was possible, of course, but what a future!

Katie decided to try some direct questions. "To have jumped out of that car like that, you must have been very frightened. Right?"

Maggie began to sob again.

"Oh, I don't want to make you cry. You don't have to tell me anything. I can see how painful it is for you to tell me what happened."

They pulled into the parking lot of the small-town grocery store. "Come, Johnny, let's get that sucker." Katie was surprised when the boy actually started following her. Maggie, right behind, also had a surprise for Katie. "We was kidnapped," Maggie said. "That's what happened."

"Oh, how awful!" exclaimed Katie, her mouth and eyes wide open. "Who ... ? What ... ?" But she realized Maggie would not know the answers. Katie could think of nothing better to say than, "Well, you're safe with me. We'll get a few groceries. Then I'll take you home."

"You not call de police?"

"I hadn't even thought about that. But, of course, I should."

"Please, Ma'am . . . , Ka-tie." Maggie shook her head violently, her eyes filled with fear. Then, lowering both head and eyes, she finally said softly, "I-I-I's skeered of de police."

"Well then," Katie reassured her, "I see no need to call them. It's not your fault you were kidnapped, and you shouldn't suffer any more than you already have. I'm here to help you."

Maggie's face brightened, and for the first time Katie could see how pretty she was. The three of them entered the store and went down aisle after aisle. Sensing they could use more than milk, Katie filled the cart with canned meat, soups, fruits and vegetables. She added sugar and flour for good measure and topped the cart off with a few packages of cookies, a cake, and a bag of suckers, which she opened immediately and gave one to Johnny. His smile gave her a one-thousand percent return on her investment.

She paid the bill, then had the young packer carry the groceries to her car and put them into the trunk. Soon the BMW and three new friends were on their way to Lonoke.

"Ma'am, Ka-tie, you have a limp. How'd you get that?"

The pained look that crossed Katie's face made Maggie sorry she had asked the question.

"I's sorry. I's sorry."

"It's okay, Maggie. A friend once said to me that anyone who has ever been mauled by a mad dog has sensitized cells and can spot another mean one before its first growl. I have learned to do this over the years, and I know there was a mean dog with you today."

Katie smiled when she saw the perplexed look on Maggie's face.

"But to be honest with you, Maggie," she continued, "I

usually very aware of my limp. However, while I was helping you and Johnny get groceries, I forgot all about it. Maybe I should help others more often. Maybe that's the key to getting on with my life."

Maggie, uncertain how to respond, smiled as well.

Then Katie added, "I have a limp because I fell. Unlike you, I held on when I should have jumped and fled. I was stupid. You were smart."

"Me? Me smart? First time I heard that!" Maggie beamed.

"Did you know the driver of that car?" asked Katie.

"No, Ma'am, ah-h, Ka-tie. Never seen him 'fore in my life."

"How did he get you into that car then?"

"I-I-I's hitchhiking."

"Oh, dear, you shouldn't hitchhike. Especially not with a child. It's so dangerous!"

"I's going one mile. Needed milk. That's why. Needed milk for my Johnny. De man, he promised to drop me off, then zoom, goes by de store. Won't let me out. Was pulling up my skirt. Doing stuff like that, and . . . ." Maggie's voice trailed off, as she fought off tears.

"Ah," said Katie, "so now I'll have to qualify what I just said. You're *not* smart for hitchhiking, and don't ever do that again! But you *are* smart—yes, *very* smart—for escaping a harmful situation." Katie glanced over at Maggie, then warmly touched her arm and smiled. Maggie returned the smile, and Johnny, who had absorbed his mother's tense moment, if not her words, let out a squeal of joy.

When they reached Maggie's modest house, Katie helped carry bags of groceries and put them on the porch. Then she hugged Maggie and Johnny. "Remember," she said, "you're too smart ever to hitchhike again."

"Oh, yes, I's smart. Never agin," said Maggie, laughing now.

No star in heaven had ever shown brighter than those two shining faces that evening.

All the way home Katie beamed. "I was in the right place

at the right time. Who knows what that wretched man might have done to them? How brave of Maggie to have escaped such a situation! With a child even!"

As she turned onto Mt. Carmel Road, she thought of Ken for the first time. She should have called, she realized, but she had been so busy that it hadn't occurred to her. But surely, when he heard how she had helped these two people in distress, he'd understand why she'd forgotten to call him.

Ken was waiting for her as she entered the house. His voice boomed: "Where have you been?"

Katie was taken back, but pressed on with her story. "You'll never guess what happened to me on my way to the store. I may have saved the life of a mother and child tonight." Then Katie proceeded to tell Ken the whole story. How Maggie and child had hitchhiked, been picked up by a man with evil intentions, and jumped out of the passenger side of the car. How she, Katie, had gone to them, put them into her car, bought them food, and then driven them home. "They were so happy when I dropped them off," she said. "They thanked me with such wonderful smiles."

She waited for Ken's approval. Instead, his face turned an ugly crimson and he said, "What a stupid thing you did! Don't you see this could have been a setup! Lucky for you it appears that it wasn't. But even if it wasn't, what you did was stupid! If it was really a kidnapping, you should have called the police. Now look what you've done. That driver is free to terrorize another person. *You* feel happy about saving one mother and child's life, but *he*'s probably killing others right now. Many others right now! It was plain stupid what you did! Plain, plain stupid!"

"But Ken . . . ." Katie wanted to explain her actions, but Ken cut her off.

With a mouth full of knives, he continued, "I don't want to hear anything about it from you! It was a dumb thing you did! You were wrong! Wrong! Wrong!"

His hurtful words stabbed her over and over again, cutting deeply, pulverizing her heart. She dropped like a wounded deer. Fortunately, a sofa caught her.

Stab! Stab! Stab!

Again and again!

Her brain shut down as all available blood hurried to protect her injured heart. She was vaguely aware of Ken's stomping out of the house, slamming the door as he went.

Her body ached with emotional pain.

"Have to ease it! Have to ease it!" she thought, desperately.

"Some gin! Some gin!"

She stumbled over to the bar, poured herself a glass of straight gin, took a few gulps, and then added a little tonic, but no ice.

Her interior burned like a house on fire. She had to put it out! Put it out!

The gin helped. But still such fury! Fire in her internal organs. She had to put it out. Put it out!

There was no way to express her anger. Her tongue was tied. She couldn't speak up in her defense, tell Ken what she really thought of him.

Fire! Fire!

More gin! More gin!

Deep swallows! Deep swallows.

More deep swallows.... Until she felt no more.

Katie didn't know what time Ken had come home. She didn't care. She had fallen asleep on the sofa. Still drowsy, she noticed that he was now up and rummaging in the kitchen, probably looking for his juice, his coffee, his cereal, his newspaper. Ha! He'd have to get it himself. Good! She heard the cupboard door slam. Her head hurt. She heard him leave. Her head hurt.

She hoped he would wreck his car and kill himself. Yes, she hoped he would die! But in a wreck not involving anyone else. A crash into a tree. Oh, her aching head!

Aspirin! In the kitchen. She needed an aspirin! A glass of water. Oh, that's better.

She needed to call Carol. To e-mail Frank and propose the new meeting time and date. Frank. His soothing letters. His gentleness. Like ointment on her wretched life. But she couldn't call Carol now. Her head hurt too much. Later. Maybe in the afternoon.

Her head throbbed mercilessly. She had to lie down. Had to go to the bathroom. She felt sick to her stomach.

Several hours later Katie felt a little better physically, but not mentally. She wondered what she had done with that telephone number. Whoever had written that newspaper article had described her situation to a tee. It had included a telephone number "in case you ever need help." She had torn it out—for some day, "just in case." Now where had she put it?

Katie looked into her desk drawer and then behind the dust board. The piece of paper with the number wasn't there. Then she remembered. She had put it behind her driver's license in her wallet. She retrieved it and dialed the number.

"Can I help you?" The voice was warm and reassuring.

"Y-yes," Katie said. "I really do need some help." She tried to keep her voice from cracking.

"Can you tell me what happened to make you call this number today?"

"I have to be assured that . . ." Katie's voice trembled. Then she managed to get it under control. "Actually, I was wondering where I might get some counseling."

"This is an abuse hot-line. Is that the type of counseling you need?"

"Yes."

"Are you in need of services immediately? I can connect you with a counselor."

"No, not immediately. I just need someone who understands this type of thing. Maybe a support group."

"Where do you live?"

"I live in Cabot, but I could never go anywhere in this town. Maybe some other, nearby town."

"There's a support group that meets Wednesday afternoons in Beebe. How about that? Is that too far away for you?"

"No, that would be fine. Wednesday afternoons. What time?"

"They meet at one. It runs until about three o'clock or so."

"Those would be good hours for me. Where do they meet?"

"At the Beebe police station. Do you know where that is?"

"At a police station!" exclaimed Katie, startled, disappointed.

"We've held it there for two years. Why? Is something wrong?"

"Thank you," said Katie simply. "I know where it is." She hung up.

Why did she meet roadblocks in everything she tried to do? She couldn't attend a meeting in a *police* station. Ken was *terrified* of police, fearing loss of reputation. From Katie's stupid acts, of course. Anyone who recognized *her* car at a police station would conclude there was something wrong with *his* universe. She couldn't take that chance. Why couldn't they meet at a church or restaurant? Anywhere but a police station!

But, didn't Ken's attitude involve more than just loss of reputation? Was this not just another one of his many criticisms of others to make her afraid to venture into the world? To keep her under his hand. A weakling. So he could be powerful. And feed on her self-esteem.

A disturbing thought occurred to her as she analyzed the incident of the previous evening. Had she wandered too far from Ken's huge hand? She knew she had, but she didn't think she had betrayed it by acting differently around him. Had he detected a change in her? And felt she needed a good dose of "destroy-self-confidence medicine" again?

And, really, what had that disastrous wedding scene been all about? To establish their respective positions? Right from the start?

These calamitous thoughts disturbed Katie so much that she had no energy for anything else that afternoon. It wasn't until the next morning that she called Carol.

"I thought you were going to call me yesterday," said Carol. "I tried to reach you a couple of times, but nobody answered. Weren't you going to send Frank an e-mail?"

Katie decided against telling Carol that she had heard the telephone ring, but had been mentally too low to answer it. She merely said she would come over that morning to e-mail Frank.

"You should know that you have a message from Frank waiting for you," said Carol. "You might want to read it before sending your own e-mail."

"Good idea. I'll be right over."

When Carol opened the door, she exclaimed: "You look awful! What's wrong with you?"

"Thanks for the compliment! I was sick yesterday."

"With what? The flu? Or was it something you ate?"

"More like something I ate. Or drank. I'm better now. My stomach is still a little upset though."

"How about some coffee? Or tea?"

"Thanks, Carol. Nothing for me, please. I'll just print out the e-mail and then get out of your hair."

With her usual joyful anticipation, Katie retrieved and printed Frank's e-mail. She noticed that it was much shorter this time. However, she avoided reading it until she was seated at her own kitchen table.

Before long, she was wiping her eyes on her sleeve. "He thinks I'm trying to deceive him," she cried. "I would *never* do anything like that to *anyone*, much less Frank. I've come to care for him deeply. I need him in my life."

She reflected back on what had transpired the previous twenty-four hours. Ken's criticisms. Belittlement. All this because her heart had gone to others! She had turned to alcohol to ease the pain.

Her subsequent call for help and the mention of the support group meeting at a police station had sent fears throughout her body. But they were reflected fears. Ken's fears. Maybe he *was* taking over her brain, as Carol had suggested in interpreting the dream. The thought that she no longer controlled her own fears made her angry.

She had spunk once, like on her wedding night. She had planned to leave the next morning, refusing to be treated in such a way. But he knew just how to wield the knife. What had she heard once? Oh, yes, he knew how to push her buttons. He used angry words, horrible words to chop up her spirit.

She would *not* allow this to happen again. She would not run and hide under that ugly hand. "My feet are on a new path!" she declared, defiantly. She would walk forward. No, *run*! She would be strong and meet Frank! She could do this! She *would* do this!

She immediately telephoned Carol. "Remember our conversation after my horrible dream, and how I was going to suggest to Frank we meet at the barn? Well, I'm going to e-mail him that message immediately. I'll suggest we meet on the seventeenth, the night Ken will be gone. Naturally, I'll fly. I have enough cash hidden away to pay for an airline ticket, but once I get there, paying for a rental car and a motel room will take more than I have. Could you loan me $200? I'll pay you back as soon as I can. Maybe pawn some jewelry when I return."

"Wow! That's a fast decision for you to make," Carol replied. "It's not like you at all, but I like it. Sure, I'll be happy to lend you the two hundred. I'm so glad you're going, and if you have any sense in your head, you'll stay. You don't even have to pay me back if you stay."

"Oh, I couldn't stay. What about Kristine?"

"Kristine has her own life. Look, she didn't even come home from college this summer, right? She's pursuing her own life. You pursue yours!"

"What would I do there longer than one night? I guess I could visit relatives in the area. But I would need time to make plans, which I don't have right now."

"God, Katie! Do I have to spell everything out for you? Stay with Frank. Get to know him a little better. He makes you happy. Give your heart a chance."

"I'm not a damsel in distress, Carol. I don't hang my heart out like a flag to summon any man that might pass by."

"Oh, 'damsel in distress'. I bet you're referring to your limp. Get over that!"

"You're like a shark, Carol. Will you never cease your attacks on me and my limp?"

"A shark, ha! Oh God, I love it! I tell you kiddo, you're getting good!"

Katie laughed. "Who could help but love you, Carol. And now I need to send a message to Frank. It won't take me long to write it because I know exactly what I need to say. I'll be over shortly to e-mail it."

Katie wrote the following letter:

> Dear Frank,
> 
>     *I am anguished to learn that you believe I purposely deceived you. Nothing could have been further from my mind. If my hand wrote any words that gave you that impression, it was acting totally independently of my feelings. Forgive me.*
> 
>     *Please be assured that your entry into my life has meant the difference between despair and happiness. I have more*

troubles here at home than I can handle at times, but I don't want to burden you with them.

My reasons for not meeting with you to sign an agreement are painfully personal. They have nothing whatsoever to do with intentional deception. However, I can understand your doubts, especially since, with complete trust, you gave me all the information you had on our common German ancestry. Please be assured that you were not foolish. Your trust was not misplaced.

In earlier correspondence, you expressed a passion to visit the Johann Gotthard farm. You asked if I knew the people that bought the place. They are distant relatives on my mother's side of the family, the same ones that bought the farm from us.

Would you accept my humblest apologies for causing you such distress and consider meeting me at the farm? We could sign the agreement in the barn, which would almost make it seem as if our collaboration was blessed by Johann and Hans.

I know you originally told me you had off on the sixteenth. I can't get there that day, but I can make it Thursday evening, July 17. Since I'll be meeting you in Columbiana rather than Pittsburgh, I'm hopeful the evening time will be acceptable and won't interfere with your day's work.

I have reserved a seat on a flight from Little Rock to the Akron-Canton Regional Airport. Arrival time is 3:55 p.m. I'll rent a car and drive to Columbiana. I'll also make hotel arrangements near the airport because I'll need to fly back to Little Rock the next morning.

I'm sure you won't have any difficulty getting from Youngstown to Columbiana. In Columbiana, catch Route 14 west. Go about one mile. Just before the Route 11 underpass, you'll see a red barn with a white farmhouse on the left side of the road. This is the Johann Gotthard Reyher farm—which, as you indicate in your story, is still known as the Wilhelm Farm. The driveway is long and curves around the house to the barn.

If the evening of the 17th is agreeable to you, I can meet you at the barn around 6:00 p.m. No one will be home as the people who now own the farm return to Lancaster, Pennsylvania, for family reunions at this time of year. My maternal aunt and her husband live across the road and handle the farm chores while they're gone.

Please draft up an agreement regarding our book collaboration and bring it with you. I'll read it over and sign it at the barn. I am honored to have you as my writing partner.

I cried when I received your letter, Frank, for, through our e-mail correspondence, I've learned to know you as a truly exceptional person. Actually, I felt as if I knew you from your first letter, and indeed I did. You have the kindness and tenderness I loved so much in my father.
Affectionately,
Katie

Katie had the e-mail ready in a half-hour. Later, at Carol's, she kissed the diskette before putting it into the computer and sending the message.

# 12

## *THE AGREEMENT PROPOSAL*

Frank choked up as he read Katie's e-mail. He shouldn't have been so harsh with her! "That damn Bill!" he muttered. "Why did I allow him to slip that ugly worm of doubt into me?"

He reread the letter several more times. "What is this with Katie? She seems to be communicating far more than written words." Indeed, it seemed that many fettered words lurked between lines because they must be spoken, yet hid in terror for fear of being voiced.

"How much of her fear is well-founded?" he wondered. "Might her planned trip to Ohio be dangerous for her?"

While these thoughts troubled Frank, he was delighted at the prospect of meeting Katie so soon. And at the Wilhelm Farm! It couldn't get any better! He'd check his calendar at work tomorrow. Since it would take less than an hour to drive to Columbiana, even if his day was full, he could still make the 6:00 time.

He decided to inform Katie immediately that the seventeenth was fine. He could draft the agreement later.

Frank turned to his computer, clicked into word processing, and started to write. Now that the dark cloud of crisis had disappeared, his little cell batteries exploded with renewed energy.

Dear Katie,

    It breaks my heart to learn how my letter upset you. I should have known better than to accuse you of deceiving me. How could I have been so callous? Please forgive me.

    Yes, I was really down, but now my enthusiasm has reached new heights, knowing that you can and will meet with me on the evening of the seventeenth. You can't imagine how happy it makes me to learn that I will finally see you, hear your voice, and be able to put a face to your beautiful words.

    Your inspired suggestion that we meet for the first time and sign our agreement at the Wilhelm barn gives me goose pimples. I'm sure Hans and Johann are smiling in anticipation.

    In the next couple of days I will work on an agreement and then e-mail it for you to look over. Please feel free to make comments and any changes you deem fit. Computers make revisions a breeze. If we do this ahead of time, perhaps we'll have a completed text ready to sign when we meet at the barn.

    I am thrilled about seeing the farm. I have a map of Columbiana and can readily locate where Route 14 crosses Route 11. Naturally, with the present owners away, we won't be able to see the farmhouse, but do you think we might get into the barn? Wouldn't it be great to stroke the same rafters that Johann touched at one time? Just think, within the space of just a few months I will have visited Johann's home in Pleidelsheim and his farm in Columbiana. All this excitement is making me feel like a kid again!

    I was wondering if you would have time to join me for dinner after we sign the agreement. My colleague has talked about a restaurant in Columbiana, the "Dutch Haus," which he says has wonderful food. What do you think? The only thing that concerns me is that you would have to drive back after dark. Let me know how you feel about this.

*I was going to ask what you look like, but decided it doesn't matter. Your beautiful soul and character come through in your letters. And I'm sure I won't have to worry about a lot of cars pulling into that driveway at that time of day! Rental cars are usually dead give-aways. In case you get there before I do, look for my dark green Saab.*

*Katie, you can't imagine how delighted I am that you initiated this new contact. To be truthful with you, even if we weren't collaborating on a book, I'd want to meet you.*
*Affectionately,*
*Frank*

# 13

## THE WILHELM FARM

When Katie read Frank's response, such peacefulness engulfed her. It was as though she had been told that she would live, after having previously been diagnosed with incurable cancer.

Frank totally forgave her. No punishment for her mistake. He even had the strength of character to take some of the blame and to ask for forgiveness as well. An equal relationship rather than an owner/slave relationship. No wonder Frank appealed to her!

Instead of making choices for her, he asked for her decision. He treated her like a grown-up rather than a child, a kitten. It gave her such strength and ... self-confidence. Of course, that was it! That was the strength she felt coming through in his letters. Belief in oneself!

No wonder her feet had taken a new direction! She could leap like a gazelle to freedom, away from the huge-handed beast demanding to be fed.

Leap like a gazelle? Such foolish thoughts. About walking, even running away from that hand. Whom was she kidding anyway? At most, given her limp, she could hobble in a new direction.

Using toll-free numbers, she confirmed her airline reservation, then made motel reservations for the night of the seventeenth. Now she was ready to e-mail Frank and tell him everything was okay for Thursday.

But when she telephoned Carol, after three rings the answering machine came on. She left a message asking Carol to call her back.

She wondered what to wear for her first meeting with Frank. Mid-July was usually hot in Ohio. She'd need something cool, but also something that would disguise her limp. For although she had enough self-confidence to defy Ken and meet Frank, she still had the embarrassment of her limp to overcome.

She rummaged through her closet and found nothing suitable. It was not yet eleven o'clock. She'd have time to go to Dillard's, buy something off their racks of dresses, and get back home in time to draft an e-mail to Frank.

At Dillard's she went through dress after dress. Finally, she found a black cotton with red poppies. It had bare shoulders, so would be cool enough. The slightly-gathered skirt was long and skimmed her feet. Hardly a dress for strolling in a barn, but she was interested in concealing a limp.

She tried it on and it fit perfectly. She practiced walking in it. Her shoes hindered her stride. She kicked them off and walked again. Her limp was inconspicuous. She bought the dress.

And what about shoes? She couldn't go barefoot in the barn, although she had done so many times in her girlhood days. She had lots of shoes at home in the closet. Perhaps she'd find something suitable there.

As she drove home, she contemplated about shoes. She couldn't take a chance on slipping or tripping, so needed something that would function well in a barn. And on the rough and uneven grounds around the farm. On the gravel driveway. Was it still gravel? Probably. Since it was so long, it would cost a fortune to pave.

When she got home, she put on her dress, then looked into her closet for shoes.

The Sam & Libby ballets would look nice with the dress. But they were cut low on the foot. They might come off as she walked, especially if the ground was the least bit muddy that evening. And it might be, she knew, for late-afternoon rainstorms were common in Ohio in the hot summer days of July.

She tried on a pair of black skimmers. The soles were slick, making it hard to walk on the bedroom carpeting. These wouldn't do. She might slip on the many wet spots on the concrete floor where cows were milked.

Reeboks would be sturdy and certainly not slippery. She put on a pair. Her long skirt hid all but the soles of the sneakers. When she tried walking, however, their weightiness accentuated her limp.

She sat on the bed to think. "I need something light, yet with a decent sole. Nothing that will slide." Then she saw her white canvas Keds? They had a rough sole, were light, and rode high on her foot. She put them on and sauntered back and forth across the room, watching herself in the mirror. *Voilá!* Her limp was unnoticeable. The Keds worked perfectly.

She hung her new dress on a hanger and placed the Keds beneath. She wouldn't need to pack much. The dress, fresh underwear, a pair of shorts and t-shirt for the return trip, nothing more than that, except pajamas for the night.

Before leaving the closet area, she looked at the rows of high-heeled pumps she still possessed. Some would be perfect with her new dress, but she couldn't wear them. Why not throw them out? Why torment herself by keeping them around?

She knew why. About a year ago, she had piled every one of them into boxes, loaded the car, and drove to the Salvation Army's drop-off store in Jacksonville. By the time she arrived, her eyes were so red from crying that she turned around and drove back home.

"These shoes will have to walk out on their own," she

had told herself as she put them back into the closet. Or someone else would have to take them to the Salvation Army. It was as if her identity was tied up in shoe strings, and tossing one away meant the other went as well.

Her mother had been right. Katie should have made a life for herself by putting something into her brain. She could have had her degree in psychology. Could have helped others. Instead, she let her legs walk out of a perfectly good life.

Insight into her marital problem had armed her with the strength to meet Frank clandestinely. That was quite a big leap for her. Then why was she so hung up over her limp?

Ah, the embarrassment thing. The discomfort of being different. Like when she was a young girl and couldn't remain behind when her classmates lined up for a school assembly. Instead, she had gone to the bathroom rather than subject herself to that embarrassment.

And not just that! At every point she seemed to be different from her classmates. She couldn't salute the flag, couldn't go to movies, couldn't have a radio—and not to mention those awful black stockings, the black bonnet, the plain dresses she was required to wear.

It was so humbling, so endless, and all designed to take away one's self-confidence. All designed to keep one in the religion by rendering one incapable of operating in the world. Just like Ken's tactics of undermining her self-confidence so she couldn't leave.

She saw it now. Oppression. Loss of freedom. The clipping of one's wings so you couldn't fly to freedom.

What was it that Carol had said about taking away one's self-confidence? Cripples you for life! What an eye opener! An oppression cripples you by taking away your potential, your full expression. It gives you a limp by limiting your freedom. No wonder she had so much trouble accepting it.

Ken must have seen that in her right away. Her confidence

problems. What was it he said appealed to him? Her innocence, her demureness. And, by using the name "Kitten," he placed her in a subjugated station from the start.

Now that she resolved her psychological problem, what could she do about her physical predicament. Must she go through the rest of her life with it?

She could conceal her limp to a certain extent. Like in her writing, for instance. But how long could she hide behind a computer? A successful writer had to make personal appearances. Could she refuse because of her lameness? The literary world would quickly tire of a writer hitched to a computer because of a hobble.

How foolish she had become! She planned to meet Frank, yet did everything she could to conceal her limp. Why would he care about it anyway? He just wanted to collaborate on a book, to sign an agreement with her. And she stupidly thought she must hide her infirmity. What would she do tomorrow, and all the other *tomorrow's* when she would be meeting with him to work on the book?

Oh, for just one good evening with him! She'd let tomorrow take care of itself. Who was it who said, "One good day is worth a thousand tomorrow's"?

Stop this foolish speculation! He had to be involved with someone else. But, on the other hand, hadn't he said she was slipping into the spot where Sally had been?

"Get a grip on yourself, Katie!" she commanded. Even if *he* wasn't involved with someone else, *she* was! Feet could reverse direction, but the knots of marriage were not easily untied. It was time to quit thinking this way!

She wondered what Frank looked like. Maybe like one of her brothers. Or like just about anyone in her family, since they were third cousins. He was probably tall. With dark hair. That ran in the Reyher family. Not blond hair like hers. She took after Mama's family.

It really didn't matter how he looked, of course. He was

in her every essence. How could she get him out? Would she have to? Of course not. As long as they were doing a book together. But a book had to be done intellectually. And, she had to admit, he was in her *emotionally*.

She longed for freedom from those stabbing knives. For the opportunity to reveal her deepest thoughts without experiencing assaulting words, words that penetrated her spirit. For a soul-to-soul encounter. Without fear of retribution. That was what she wanted. Without this, did one have love?

Alas! she thought. There'd be just one evening with Frank. She'd show him the barn, turn on some lights, sign the agreement. Perhaps, if they had time, they'd see a little of the farm. Then they'd go to the restaurant for dinner.

She'd return to her motel room and down a sedative to get to sleep. She'd catch her plane in the morning, fly into Adams Field, and, with leaden legs and numbed feelings, get into her car and drive back to her cage.

Frank would return home to Youngstown and do whatever it was he did. He'd never know about her limp, about her imprisoned life.

At least they'd have the book to do. They'd still e-mail each other. She'd continue to receive those comforting letters, to which she had become addicted.

But what if they sold the book? Those personal appearances! She wouldn't be able to make them. He'd have to go for her. What excuse would she use? She remembered what Mama had said: "Start down a path of lies and deceit, soon briers and thorns will bind your feet."

The telephone rang. It was Carol. Katie told her she'd be right over to e-mail Frank a short message.

Katie composed the message on-line. She wrote that she had confirmed plane and hotel reservations for Thursday, the seventeenth, and would be returning on the eighteenth. That it would be most fitting for them to have dinner at Dutch Haus, a restaurant with good "German Mennonite" cuisine, for she was aware of the restaurant's reputation. And, that she was *not* afraid to drive at night and *was* familiar with the roads.

She asked him to draft an agreement and e-mail it to her. She agreed it was a good idea to have any difficulties worked out beforehand so that they could sign the agreed text at the barn. She assured him they would have no difficulty getting into the barn since people in the Columbiana area never saw a need to lock them.

In conclusion, she relayed to him how delighted she was that they would finally meet. She closed the letter with "affectionately."

On the 17th, Katie drove to Adams Field and boarded her plane. Her luggage was minimal: one carry-on. The day was cloudless, and the flight went so well that she arrived at Akron-Canton a few minutes early. She checked into renting a car and chose the least expensive one available. She let them take an imprint of her credit card, but, in the end, she would pay for it in cash.

It was a few minutes drive to Hampton Inn. She checked in and, before doing anything else, hung up the dress. She noted with relief that it was unwrinkled. She laid out her underwear and shoes, then took a shower. She lathered herself generously with White Diamonds shower gel, then took such deep breaths the fragrance shifted her spirits into a sexy level. She got out, dried off, then looked at herself in the mirror. Despite her forty-five years, her figure was perfect, her breasts and hips taut. She congratulated herself on good genes, for she knew that none of this was due to disciplined exercise or diet.

She suddenly noticed she had packed the wrong bra. She needed a strapless one. Why hadn't she thought of that? She wondered if she'd have time to shop before meeting Frank.

She looked at the dress again. Lucky for her it was double bodiced! She slipped it on and it fit well. The dress brushed against her bare nipples, causing them to perk up. She felt it, but when she looked in the mirror, the bodice was thick enough to hide it.

Next, her panties, and then her Keds. She practiced walking as she watched in the mirror. She could not detect a limp.

Finally, she applied a little rouge, mascara, and eyebrow pencil, then brushed her long blond hair over her back, which she French braided. One last practice-walk in front of the mirror. Then a vivacious strut. Perfect. She locked the room and headed for her car.

She began the drive to Columbiana. It would take about an hour to get there, maybe a little less. There would be plenty of time to see the barn. Maybe there would be enough daylight for them to walk around the outside of the farmhouse as well. Maybe they should walk around the farmhouse first, saving the barn for later. After all, they could always turn on the lights in the barn.

Her heart pounded as she thought about meeting Frank. "Good grief!" she scolded. "You're acting like a silly school girl. Get a grip on yourself!"

When Katie arrived, a green Saab was nowhere in sight. As she drove up the long driveway, the farmhouse where she had been born and raised came into view. Her heart warmed recalling those wonderful days.

There were rows and rows of mixed flowers, just like she had planted when she was a child. Katie grinned broadly, recalling her mother's saying that flowers were God's smiles on earth.

She followed the driveway very slowly as it curved by the farmhouse. The green Saab came into view. It was parked near the barn.

She slapped her chest to quiet her pounding heart, hoping, somehow, to reset its pace. She wondered how defibrillators worked so well.

The door of the Saab was open, with Frank in a bright sport shirt standing alongside. He was deep in thought, his hand cupping his chin, as he looked at the barn.

She immediately noticed that he was tall. And thin. With a shock of straight, dark hair that fell disobediently over his face. Her heart leaped.

A late-afternoon breeze tousled Frank's hair, leaving a few stand upright. He brushed them down. A frisky twirl uprighted another strand. She was amused. It gave him a school-boy look. To go with her school-girl feelings.

She smacked her face. Stop this nonsense!

Then Frank heard her car approach. He shut his Saab door and turned in her direction. She could see his broad smile, his mouth full of gleaming, white teeth. When she stopped, he strode over quickly, opened the door and extended his hand. "Hi Katie. Thank heavens you're here! It's wonderful to meet you at last. Here, let me help you out of the car."

"It's okay, Frank, I can get out on my own," she said. She turned her body forty-five degrees so that her feet and legs hung over the open doorway, then eased them to the ground. She pulled at her skirt to make sure it discreetly hid her Keds. Only then did she reach out and accept Frank's hand. He closed the door gently behind her.

"I know you're not late, Katie, but I was still concerned about you. My head and my heart don't always coordinate very well. I was wondering how your flight went, whether maybe you'd had trouble getting here."

For Katie, Frank's words were a reminder of his e-mails. He opened himself up. Made himself vulnerable. Shared what he was thinking. In the flesh as well, he was a person with secure feelings about himself.

"My flight went well. I even arrived a little earlier than anticipated. I had plenty of time to freshen up and change clothes at the motel. How about your drive?"

"I had no problem. I got off a little early. Neglected my after-hours paperwork, which is not a good habit to get into. I like what you changed into. That's a beautiful dress."

Katie, remembering she was braless, blushed, then changed the subject. "This farm brings back so many fond memories," she said, pointing toward the road. "Did you happen to notice the rows of flowers as you made the first turn in the driveway? It was my job to plant them when I was a child. Remember, I wrote that to you once."

"Not only do I remember, Katie, I actually stopped and smelled them. I thought how right your mother was. Flowers are God's smiles."

"Oh, you remember my writing that?"

"I remember everything you wrote. I won't forget any of your words.

"This farm is gorgeous," Frank continued. "I got here about ten minutes ago and walked around a little. I am captivated by its history, by the fact that Johann Gotthard once walked on the very ground where we now stand. It humbles me, yet stimulates me."

"Me too, when I stop to think about it. What should we see first, the barn or the farmhouse?" asked Katie.

"I want to see as much as I can before it gets dark, and especially the barn that our great-great-grandfather must have known so well. And, of course, your father and you too."

"We could walk around the farmhouse while there is still daylight." But then Katie, remembering how far she'd have to walk, *limp*, quickly added, "No. Let's see the barn first. As we drive out, we can walk around the farmhouse. Dutch Haus closes at eight, and we should be out of here by seven at the latest. It will still be light enough at that hour to see the farmhouse."

"Also, with no clouds in the sky, I'm sure the full moon will provide plenty of light for us. Katie, I'm your guest. Lead the way."

"To the barn it is then. Let's go in this side door. It will take us to the milking area. Of course, the cows will have been milked and sent out to pasture. This door will also give us access to the rest of the barn. Even to the straw and haylofts. There's a ladder leading to them. I'll let you go up there alone. I don't think I could climb that ladder in this skirt."

"I'll bet you didn't wear a dress like that when you came to the barn as a young girl," Frank teased. Then he quickly added, "But I'm glad you wore it for me. You look great in it.

"It's in such nice shape," said Frank, pointing to the barn they approached. "Has it changed much over the years?"

"I was told the outside is pretty much like it was originally, but the inside has been altered to keep up with the times. When I milked cows, it was all done by hand. Now it's done by machine. Improvements have been made to keep up with new developments in the dairy industry."

Frank tried the door. "It's locked!"

"I can't believe it," said Katie. "We *never* locked our barn doors. Let's try the door that leads directly to the hay loft."

Just then a cow mooed in the meadow. Katie turned in the direction of the sound and took a few steps over to the fence. Frank was quickly at her side, and quietly they drank in the beauty of a enchanting early-evening pasture scene. Fields and meadows played soft music as they told their last stories of the day. Daytime creatures sang sweet lullabies to their little ones, then invited the sun to lovingly tuck them into beds. It had been a tiring day for the sun, with not a cloud to give him rest. And as soon as he got everyone into bed, he eagerly turned over his job to the moon—who was responsible for the care of nighttime creatures.

"It's a wonderful sight, Katie, so much more than I could ever have imagined. Look over there! Is that the cornfield you told me about?"

Katie gasped. "Oh, yes, it is! And look! Freshly tilled!"

Katie forgot all about her limp and hobbled as fast as she could toward it.

Frank stared at her. Then, two plus two became four as he understood for the first time. This was not a limp from birth, in which the bearer and limp had become one. This limp was recently acquired and not assimilated into the owner's identity.

He followed Katie. Soon she was hidden by the high stalks of corn, but he had seen the row she had taken. When he caught up with her, she was already lying face-up between two rows.

"Come on," she said. "Come lie by my side. You'll never believe how good this makes your body feel."

"I have a blanket in my car. I'll be right back."

"Oh, no, don't! You won't get the earth's nutrition through a blanket. You have to lie upon the soil, and it's best when freshly tilled and raked. It's very therapeutic, renews your spirit. Come on. Try it!

"I did this many times when I was young, whenever my spirit needed nourishment. It always made me feel good. Still does. Just lying here on this dirt. Looking up at the sky. I can feel the nourishment rising from the earth and entering me. Deep into my body. Don't you want to try it?"

Frank laughed. "You might have developed a liking for it, Katie. I don't think I'm there yet. I'll get the blanket." He soon returned with a blanket and knelt by Katie's side. She detected a slight medicinal odor.

Katie looked so content that Frank was sure she had satiated herself on the earth's nutrition. He gently lifted her head, undid her braid, and then with his fingers combed the dirt out of her hair. He lifted her bare shoulders, then her body, carefully spreading the blanket beneath her. Finally he lifted her legs and smoothed the blanket beneath them. He removed her shoes and looked at her foot. It was obviously some kind of injury that she had suffered. Very gently he placed her feet on the blanket and then lay beside her.

"Katie," he said, turning toward her and resting on his left elbow. "I saw you limp. My profession requires me to look beyond the obvious. I think I know why you wore your long skirt tonight. I think I also know why you made all those excuses for not meeting me. You didn't want me to know, did you?"

Katie's only response was a little sniffle.

"I looked at your foot. At some point you suffered an injury that wasn't properly handled. Want to tell me what happened?"

Katie's eyes filled with tears.

Frank leaned over her face and kissed her tears. "Katie," he said tenderly, "I'm not asking you this because it's going to make a difference in how I feel about you. I knew your core long before I saw you. I knew you were beautiful inside. And now that I see you, you're gorgeous on the outside as well.

"The reason I asked about your foot is because I think I may be able to help you."

Tears ran down Katie's cheeks.

Frank sat up and searched his pockets for a handkerchief. Realizing he had forgotten to take one, he removed his sport shirt. "Sorry," he said with a sheepish smile. "All I have is this."

"Thanks," Katie said, dabbing the tears carefully. When she finished, she buried her face in the shirt. She liked the smell. She took several deep breaths. The odor was a mixture of tenderness and virility, soothing yet stimulating, a powerful elixir. It gave her the strength she needed to talk, to tell Frank about her deep hurt.

She removed his shirt from her eyes, but kept it over her nose. Then she took more deep breaths. She searched his deep blue eyes with hers. He was a man who would understand.

"First, I want you to know," Katie sobbed, "it was all my fault. It was foolish of me to try to grab that door handle."

Frank stroked her brow and wiped her tears with the sleeve of his shirt. His eyes encouraged her to continue.

"It happened about two years ago." She felt stronger, more confident.

"Ken and I had attended a fund-raising banquet at the Excelsior. That's a luxury hotel in downtown Little Rock. We were on our way home when he asked if I would like to stop at the Happy Tequila bar in North Little Rock for a drink. It sounded like a nice way to finish off the evening.

"There were empty tables around the room, but since we hadn't planned to stay long, we sat at the bar. The bar was crowded, with only two seats left. We took them. It just so happened that seated on my left was a good-looking guy. I just noticed it, certainly nothing more than that." Katie sighed.

Frank took his shirt from Katie and rolled it up into a pillow. He gently lifted her head and, after smoothing her hair, placed the pillow under it. He arranged her blond locks carefully across her bare shoulders.

Her sigh told him the story would be more difficult beyond this point. He kissed her cheek, then said, "I'm listening. What happened next?"

"We ordered gin and tonics. I did tell you this was my fault, didn't I?"

"Yes, you did. You ordered gin and tonics."

"It didn't take us long to down those, as we were pretty thirsty. Then we ordered another round. The bartender set those drinks before us and everything was just fine, when. . . . ."

"When what, Katie? You can tell me," he said gently as he stroked her hair, her shoulders, her arms.

Katie caught her breath and began again. "Everything was fine, and we were talking. I looked up at myself in the mirror behind the bar and unintentionally caught the eye of the good-looking guy sitting to my left. I quickly looked at Ken to see if he had noticed. Experience over the years led me to take that precaution, I guess. Anyhow, Ken was looking at me in the mirror and apparently had seen everything, because his eyes were full of fire."

Katie sighed, "It's so hard for me to go on."

"I know this is difficult, Katie, but you'll feel much better if you tell me. I suspect you've never told anyone this before. You need to get it out."

Katie was strengthened by Frank's encouraging words. He was right. She never *had* told anyone before. Not even Carol.

"It's always dangerous when I see fire in Ken's eyes," she continued. "It means he's out of control."

"You're safe with me, Katie. You can tell me everything."

"Ken threw his drink in my face, then reached into his pocket and pulled out a twenty-dollar bill. 'Here!' he said, angrily throwing it at the bartender. 'That should take care of the b-b-b . . . ' It's really hard for me to say that word."

"But you should say it, Katie. Get all of that out of you. It's been lurking within you much too long."

"I know I need to. The word is b-b-bitch. He said 'the bitch's bill.' He stomped out of the bar."

"Katie," said Frank. "It wasn't your fault, not your fault at all that you happened to be looking in that mirror when someone else did at the same time. Everybody's done that. It's a blameless thing to do." He snuggled closer.

"That part wasn't my fault," said Katie. "I know I was innocent there. But it set him off. I never know why it happens, but it's like a firestorm in his brain. I have to be so careful."

"Did he just leave you there? To find your own way home?"

"He would have. But after I wiped the drink out of my eyes, I came to my senses. I realized that was exactly what he intended to do. I ran out of the bar just as he got into the car. He started the engine. I ran as fast as I could and made it to the car. I reached for the door handle and . . ." Katie openly sobbed again.

Frank took a corner of the blanket and wiped her tears. "Go ahead, Katie, tell me what happened next."

"It's just so hard to relive it," she sobbed.

Frank dried her eyes again, then kissed them very gently. "I know it is, but you can tell me, Katie. Get it all out of you."

"I-I-I grabbed the car door handle. The car. It was *moving*." She sniffed a couple of times and seemed unable to go on.

"The car was moving. Then what happened?" Frank's voice made her feel safe enough to continue.

"It knocked me down."

"To the ground? The pavement, Katie? Onto the pavement?"

"Yes. The pavement. My leg. The side was all scraped. My hip. It hurt terribly."

"And your foot? What happened to your foot, Katie."

"My leg and hip hurt so badly, I didn't even realize I'd hurt my foot. At least not at that time."

"Did Ken just leave you there like that?"

"No. He wheeled the car around to where I was, half-lying, half-kneeling. He opened the door and told me, 'Get in, bitch!' Can you believe it? I actually got in. I crawled into that car after he called me 'bitch.'"

"What choice did you have? Don't be so hard on yourself. You did nothing wrong. So, you went home?"

"He took me home. We didn't say one word to each other. Nothing. After I got out of the car, I dragged myself toward the house. He backed out of the driveway and left. I don't know where he went."

"Didn't you go to the doctor? You should have gone to the emergency room! That very night!"

"I didn't. I couldn't. I hurt too badly. It wasn't the physical pain that kept me from going. I was too *ashamed* to go. My side, my leg all scraped up. And my foot was really beginning to swell. I could barely walk, it was so swollen. I should have called for help, but what was I to tell them? There might have been a police report."

"Did you go to the doctor the next day?"

"I was too embarrassed. Like I said, it was my fault."

"It wasn't your fault. Did you *ever* go to the doctor?"

"Yes, a couple of weeks later, but it was too late. He x-rayed and said I had broken a bone in my foot. One of those foot bones, I forget the name. But by that time, it was too late. And now, this limp. I'll be forever reminded of that night. My foolishness." Katie shook with sobs.

So much for *sticks and stones may break my bones, but words will never hurt me*, thought Frank. But he knew that a clever turn of phrase was not what Katie needed to hear at that moment. Instead, he took her in his arms and gently rocked her.

Then he said, "Katie, I am a doctor. An orthopedic surgeon at St. Elizabeth's. I can make you walk properly again. You don't have to have your limp forever. Will you trust me?"

He felt her body shiver, like someone coming out of a high fever. He wrapped her tightly in his arms until the shaking subsided. He kissed her hair, her lips. "I love you, Katie. I know now I've loved you from your very first letter to me, maybe even before that. I felt totally connected with you when I read the summary of your story on the elderly woman and the butterflies."

He kissed her passionately.

"I've never felt like this since Sally's death. Come home with me. Come to where it's safe. I've sensed in your letters that you are afraid of Ken."

"I am," said Katie. "I've been afraid of him since our wedding night."

"Don't live with someone you fear. That can only mean oppression, which makes happiness impossible. We're both Reyher descendants. Look at the oppression our ancestors have known. Look at Hans. He fled the oppression of primogeniture for a better life. Johann fled an oppressive mercenary system. I too have known oppression, one self-inflicted in a way. I was not free because of my inability to put my wife's death into perspective. Your own father fought an oppressive disease."

Katie sniffled. "Papa was brave. I want to be like him. I tried to be brave once."

"You can be brave again, but everybody's oppression is different. Yours involves living in fear of your own husband. You don't *fight* that kind of oppression with bravery. You *flee* it, just as Hans and Johann did. And you're a heron. You can do it." He kissed her lips again, her cheeks, her neck.

He looked into her eyes. "Katie, you shouldn't live with someone you're afraid of. What are you going to do when you return? How are you going to explain your absence? Won't Ken be furious with you?"

"He's gone on a one-night business trip. I don't think he'll know that I'm gone."

"So that's why you made this a one-day trip. You have to hurry back before he finds out you came to sign an agreement with me, right? You're going to end up badly hurt, Katie. Come home with me. Tell you what. Let's make this the 'Flight of the Heron III.'"

Katie laughed and cried at the same time. "I'd like that," she said. Then she looked into his eyes and Frank felt her cells all turn his way: accepting him—requesting him.

He held her close. The thumping of his heart matched hers. Then Katie said words that came from so deep within her body that they shocked her mouth. "I've loved you from your first letter, Frank. I love you very much."

She kissed him passionately. "I know I'm safe with you."

"Will you come home with me then, Katie?"

"On my wedding day, I admired a bluebird because he had wings and was free. I am a heron. I can be free. I will fly away with you to your nest."

# FLIGHTS OF THE HERONS

Frank and Katie again kissed passionately. Then . . .

With eyes opened wide, the full moon on high
Zoomed in on this little piece of July.
Said he'd tell Mr. Sun, at least this was his reason,
That although he'd been tired, this was hardly the season,
That it just wasn't smart to have shucked this sunset,
But put toothpicks in eyes, which had hurt no one yet,
And stayed up to see this cornfield consummation,
For shuteye was no match for this happy occasion,
For truly this was a pleasure to behold,
And it might be a while, well if truth be told,
Bliss such as this he'd not witness soon,
And who should know better that he, Mr. Moon,
Who thought it'd be years 'fore he'd see it again,
And oh, goodness, oh goodness, oh goodness, ohhhhh.
Mr. Sun could work all day long if he liked;
The moon knew the best time to work was the night.

Frank and Katie were unaware of the moon's vicarious behavior, for their eyes were closed in joyous pleasure as cells intermeshed in a climax of body and soul.

Exhausted but exhilarated, Katie and Frank lay on the blanket, arm-in-arm, and quietly enjoyed the constellations in the northern sky: Cassiopeia, Cepheus, the Little Dipper, and the Big Dipper.

After some time, Frank said, "I can't believe how beautiful a country sky truly is. We city boys never get to witness so many magnificent stars in a sky uncrowded by other lights. It's awesome to think that Hans and Johann enjoyed these same stars and the full moon."

Then Katie teased, "Do you think Hans and Johann approve of our union?"

Frank laughed. "They probably arranged it."

He then turned to Katie and said, "Seriously, ever since I

learned you were a writer and related to me, I have wondered why our paths might have crossed. Was it due to fate or chance? And why? I couldn't believe it was simply to write a book together. Now I know why our paths crossed."

"Why is that, Frank?"

"I was sent to rescue you from Ken's oppression and to free you from your limp. You were sent to rescue me from my oppression, that of loneliness and an inability to get over Sally's death."

"That's a wonderful way of putting it, Frank. But one thing: Who *sent* us?"

"I think it was Hans and Johann. I think our ancestors had a hand in this."

"So that means it was purposeful, an act of fate."

"I haven't resolved that question yet. It appears there were too many coincidental circumstances for it to have happened as a result of sheer chance. But fate? I'm not sure I'd really say it was due to fate either."

Katie laughed. "Tell you what, Frank. First let's write this heron book together. Then we'll collaborate on a book about fate and chance. Maybe we can come up with an answer."

"We may collaborate together for life," laughed Frank.

"I hope so," said Katie. Then she remembered the agreement. "We haven't signed the agreement yet. We were going to do so in the barn."

"Tell you what," teased Frank. "Why don't I just hold it up to the moon and have it signed by Hans and Johann."

"Signed via the moonlight by two dead ancestors. Sounds like a perfectly legal agreement to me," laughed Katie.

They were silent for a few moments as they took in the marvelous night sky display. Then Katie said, "I could lie here forever, but I have to admit, I'm hungry. I think we've missed dinner at the Dutch Haus by several hours. Do you know of any places open at this time of night where we could get something to eat?"

"How about some pizza and wine at my house?"

"I'd love that."

"I have a cell phone in the car. I'll call and order now. By the time we get to my house, it should be arriving." Frank made the telephone call.

Frank kissed Katie tenderly. "Ready to fly, Heron?"

"I'm ready."

"Do you have a cell phone in your car?"

"No, but I have one in my purse."

"Well, let me give you my number and you can give me yours. That way if we lose each other, we can communicate."

"Sounds like a wonderful idea. I have a note pad in my purse." She wrote down Frank's number, tore it off and put it on her dashboard. Then she wrote down her number and gave it to Frank.

"I'm your guest," said Katie. "Lead the way."

"Don't forget to turn on your cell phone," Frank said, as he got into his car.

They had been on the road less than fifteen minutes when Katie's cell phone rang. "Frank must be calling me," she thought.

"Hi Frank," she answered.

"Frank? Who's Frank? This is Ken."

Katie froze when she heard his voice.

"Where *are* you? I tried to call you at home, but there was no answer, so I decided to try your cell phone."

She remembered the "end" button and quickly stilled his tongue. She dialed Frank's number.

"Hi Frank. Do you see that little bridge you're just about to cross. Well, I'm going to pull over there. I need to throw something into the river."

"What's that, Katie?"

"My cell phone. You'll never guess who just called. I hung up on him, though."

Katie heard Frank's chuckle.

"A heron learning to use her wings should not be shackled to objects from her past."

She heard Frank chuckle again, then say, "You're flying well, heron. See you at my nest."

The End

Printed in the United States
2951